Praise for
Daisy Chains

"Sandra Byrd has written an honest story about the implications of making your faith your own that young people will readily identify with. . . . I am especially thankful for this book because there is relatively little material about Messianic Jewish believers that is written with skill and care and is culturally authentic. This story admirably will help begin to fill that gap, and I hope that it will encourage young people, both Jewish and Gentile, to examine the claims of Jesus as Messiah for themselves. Sandra does this without preaching, with dialogue that is real, with characters that you care about, and through a very engaging and enjoyable story that I found hard to put down."

—Janie-sue Wertheim
Children's and Youth Minister,
Jews for Jesus

Books by
Sandra Byrd
FROM BETHANY HOUSE PUBLISHERS

Girl Talk
Chatting With Girls Like You
A Growing-Up Guide
The Inside-Out Beauty Book
Stuff 2 Do

FRIENDS FOR A SEASON
Island Girl
Chopstick
Red Velvet
Daisy Chains

THE HIDDEN DIARY
Cross My Heart
Make a Wish
Just Between Friends
Take a Bow
Pass It On
Change of Heart
Take a Chance
One Plus One

FRIENDS for a SEASON

DAISY CHAINS

Sandra Byrd

BETHANYHOUSE
MINNEAPOLIS, MINNESOTA

Published by Bethany House Publishers
11400 Hampshire Avenue South
Bloomington, Minnesota 55438

Bethany House Publishers is a division of
Baker Publishing Group, Grand Rapids, Michigan.

Printed in the United States of America

ISBN-13: 978-0-7642-0023-6
ISBN-10: 0-7642-0023-2

Library of Congress Cataloging-in-Publication Data

Byrd, Sandra.
    Daisy chains / by Sandra Byrd.
        p.   cm. — (Friends for a season)
        Summary: "Two girls, cousins of a bride and groom—one Jewish, one not—learn that friendship reaches beyond religion. And they discover they have a lot to learn about faith, too"—Provided by publisher.
    ISBN 0-7642-0023-2 (pbk.)
    [1. Friendship—Fiction. 2. Interpersonal relations—Fiction.
3. Religion—Fiction. 4. Jews—United States—Fiction. 5. Christian life—Fiction.] I. Title.

    PZ7.B9898 Di   2006
    [Fic]—dc22

                                    2005032034

For Jesus
For Michael
He loves me

SANDRA BYRD lives near Seattle with her husband, two children, and a tiny Havanese circus dog named Brie. Besides writing *Island Girl* and the other FRIENDS FOR A SEASON books, Sandra is the bestselling author of the SECRET SISTERS SERIES, THE HIDDEN DIARY SERIES, and the nonfiction book collection GIRLS LIKE YOU.

Learn more about Sandra and her books at *www.friendsforaseason.com.*

CHAPTER ONE
kylie's story

Love in a Mist *Nigella damascene*
This is a charming Victorian plant. It blooms in watercolor shades, but usually periwinkle blue. It reseeds itself year after year from pods formed during the blooming season.

—Northwest Gardener's Guide

"Love in a Mist" is also what could happen if you live in Seattle, where it rains all the time, and a cute guy you don't even know knocks on your door and hands you a book and a mysterious invitation. I know. It happened to me!

—Kylie Peterson

I twirled a spoon in my breakfast cereal, catching a cornflake and then slurping it into my mouth as I read the comics. My mom never read the paper that she paid for; someone might as well. I checked my watch. Fifteen minutes till the bus.

"Hayley! Hurry up!" I shouted, never taking my eyes from the paper.

The article printed next to Dear Abby caught my eye. "Teens Need Independence and Excitement!" A list followed and I skimmed it.

I was too young to drive a motorcycle, so that was unfortunately out.

New and unusual hairstyle. Got it. I had been braiding my hair into tiny braids at night for a few weeks, shaking out wavy kinks each morning.

A first love. Too bad I'd already checked out the pickings and found them wanting. Besides, my mother had effectively nixed boyfriends till I was seventeen.

Something important to believe in. Oh yes. How I wanted that, something that was permanent, dependable, trustworthy. But what?

One thing on the list *would* work for me: a summer job. In fact, I'd already applied.

I licked my lips, exhaled, and pleaded, *Please, God, let the one and only summer job I could have come through.* I'd been checking the mail every day all week looking for the envelope, which still had not arrived.

I crossed out the word *Teens* on the article and overwrote my name in big, bold letters. "**KYLIE** Needs Independence and Excitement." Then I cut the article out and went to check on my sister.

"Here, let me help."

Hayley swatted me away. She was trying to fix her hair with one hand; her left arm was in the smudged sling we kept in the closet for her every-other-month trauma.

I heard the bus gears grind and rushed her. "Hurry! Your bus just turned into the neighborhood!"

Hayley squawked at me and I squawked back, but we hobbled out in enough time for her to make her bus and for me to get to mine. I sat on my seat with my iPod cranking and thought. I was going to make some of the things on that list happen, somehow.

Later that morning, between second and third period, I headed to the eighth-grade lockers, like always, to meet up with Sarah so we could walk to class.

"Kylie!" Sarah called out to me. She looked anxious.

"What's up?"

"Hear anything?"

Now it was my turn to be anxious. "Nope. Did you?"

She nodded her head. "I got the letter yesterday."

"And. . . ?"

"And I got a space!" Sarah couldn't hide her smile, and I wouldn't have wanted her to. "The first training isn't till next month. But they want the commitments back soon. I—I should wait for you to get your letter first. Before mailing in my commitment, that is."

I took a deep breath. I'd had lots of practice hiding my emotions so no one would know the conversations inside my head and my heart. Not even my best friend.

"No! Send it in right away. Don't wait for me." I slammed my locker door shut and locked it. "What more perfect summer job could there be? You only have to work six hours a day, and you get to job-share with a friend."

Sarah chimed in, "And every weekend there are team parties with other teens and mud pit games and rock climbing and riding. And we'll get paid!"

We'll get paid. But *we* don't both have the job yet. I rustled up enthusiasm and told her, "Send that letter back, girl!"

We walked into third period, language arts, and slid into cool melamine seats next to each other. "Sarah?" I asked softly as I took out a pen and notebook.

"Yeah?"

"Do you think they might leave me out because I don't go to your church?"

She shook her head. "No. Even though my church sponsors the camp, the counselors can be Christians from any Bible-teaching church. So don't worry."

Bible-teaching church? Hmm. I'd never heard that phrase before. I think we read the Bible at my grandpa's church, which was, I suppose, *my* church. I mean, what else did you teach in church besides the Bible?

Ms. Wamba called us to attention and class began. My letter would probably be there when I got home today.

Or not.

Hayley's bus got home right after mine. The elementary school day was half an hour longer than the middle school day. Mom felt good that Hayley wasn't alone, and Hayley was glad I was there to meet her. I felt good to be useful.

Hayley got off of the bus, her barrettes sliding down the slopes of her temples, one shoe untied but a smile on her face. She still had her sling on. Yikes. At least she wasn't toting her fake inhaler, too. She hadn't had any health problems, fake or otherwise, at all until my dad up and left us three years ago.

"So how was your day, kiddo?" I hitched up my

backpack. They'd laid on the work the last couple of months with homework almost every night.

"Good. Do I have ballet today?"

Mental check. Friday. "Yep." I scanned the street for upraised mail flags and saw none. *Mail must have already come.*

"It's April Fool's Day," Hayley said. "I planned some pranks at school today. One good one I hope Mom will fall for."

"If she's home in time." My mom worked late almost every day at a powerful advertising firm in downtown Seattle. April Fool's Day or not, her schedule was no joke.

"I'm going to make her bed over tonight—but I'll fix the sheets so they only go halfway down the bed." Hayley grinned and I did, too.

At the mailbox I tugged on the handle, then reached into the cave of the box. Two bills, a magazine for my mother, three credit card offers—unfortunately none of them addressed to me. I'd love my own credit card.

Wait. Here it was. I recognized the name of Sarah's church in the return address.

"You go inside," I said to Hayley. "Go on, let the dog out of her crate and get a snack. I'll be right there."

She hopped up the driveway and I walked slowly, tucking the other mail under my arm and slitting the back of the envelope.

"Dear Miss Kylie Peterson," it read. "We are happy to tell you that you have been assigned a spot on our summer staff. You will be a Junior Counselor, working together with a Senior Counselor and another Senior/Junior team with second-grade girls. Our first staff training will be in May. . . ."

"YES!" I stopped reading right there. I'd made it! And I wouldn't even be counseling Hayley's grade. She was a good kid, you know, but we could use a break from each other.

I pushed the door open, flicked my flip-flops off right inside the door, and shut the door with my painted-blue big toe, still reading the paper in my shaking hand.

"Please send this letter of intent back within two weeks so we'll know how many counselors we can count on. By signing the bottom of the page, you acknowledge that you have *been a Christian for at least one year, attend your church regularly*, and are *seeking to grow in your faith*."

Then the camp director signed it. A stamped, self-addressed envelope was included.

I had never heard language like that; it was kind of weird. *A Christian for at least one year?* What would that mean, that I was at least two years old—I mean, wasn't I born a Christian just like everyone else in my family?

Attend my church regularly?

Hayley called from the kitchen. "I'm eating Oreos. Then we'd better walk to ballet. I'll get in trouble if I'm late."

I entered the kitchen to find the table peppered with black cookie crumbs like ants at a picnic. I pulled a frozen entrée out of the freezer and put it into the oven. Then I looked out the back window. It was clouding over, starting to drizzle a little. Seattle sunshine. "Let's go," I said. "Take the sling off, or Miss Tikka won't let you into ballet."

Hayley slipped the sling off, and I glanced at the letter one more time, heart racing. Would Sarah know what that strange language meant?

Nah. Her family already seemed so perfect next to mine, I didn't want her thinking we were weird in other ways, too.

"It probably means nothing." I said the words out loud to myself as I flipped open my phone to call her. I was a real believer that saying words out loud would convince me—and others—that they were true. Sometimes it worked, sometimes it didn't. Hey, if it didn't, I could shove my doubts into a mental closet and close the door. I was good at that, too.

I reached into the dryer to take Hayley's leotard out and tossed it to her while waiting for Sarah to pick up. Sarah's voice mail came on. "My letter came!" I shouted into the phone. "What grade are you leading? I'm second grade. Maybe we're teamed up. Call me back. Bye!"

Next I called my mom while Hayley struggled into her leotard in the downstairs bathroom.

"Hi, Mom. We're home."

"That's good, honey. How was your day?"

"Really, really good. I got accepted for the summer job!"

"Hooray!" My mom's enthusiasm crackled through the phone line. "You always do everything so well, Kyls; I just knew they'd offer it to you. Why wouldn't they want a lovely young lady like you? Especially with all of your child-care experience."

"It's not child care, Mom. I'm a camp counselor."

"I know, honey. I am just so pleased for you. What with your having to watch Hayley during the summer, there aren't really any other jobs that would work for us. With this job, she can go too! Are you on your way to ballet?"

"Yep, and I started dinner. It should be ready when you get here."

"I might be a little late. If I don't finish this deal up before I leave today, I'm dead," Mom said. "I'll call and let you know. I'm very proud of you. Let me say hello to Hayley and then get back to work."

Hayley yammered on while I grabbed a Mountain Dew from the fridge, went back to the window, looked at the drizzle, and decided it wasn't so bad that we would need an umbrella to walk the few blocks to the dance studio. Just as I was about to turn away, I saw a silver truck drive by slowly. I didn't recognize it, but what really caught my eye is that it slowed way down, kind of in front of my house. I thought it was going to stop. Instead, the truck took off again. It looked like there was a guy in it, a teenage guy. What was he doing stopping in front of our house?

I shrugged. Maybe he was a delivery guy looking for an address.

I stuck the job offer envelope on the ledge where we kept the mail and headed out the door with Hayley. *Aahhh*. I was on my way to a summer of parties, fun, cash, and coolness. I was even excited to learn more about God. Ever since Sarah and I became friends, that was kind of a new interest. I'd even gone to church with Grandpa. When he'd take me. Which wasn't, um, regularly.

That last line from the letter sounded strange, too. *"Seeking to grow in your faith"*? I didn't know anyone who talked like that.

We walked the few blocks to Miss Tikka's dance studio. I took a book and my Dew and my phone, lazing outside of Hayley's first-grade dancers' classroom while she did ballet. The little girls looked like marionettes, bopping and dipping and swirling with

Miss Tikka, stretching their little legs on a bar. They were so cute.

I walked down the hall to throw my can away. Well, I did have to throw the can away, but I also wanted to peek in on another class. A hip-hop class. Girls my age getting a great workout and having a good time dancing. I felt my feet tapping out the rhythm. I *loved* to dance, but I'd never done anything kind of, well, free. Goofy maybe. Everyone always told me how mature I was. But I kind of envied the girls in that class who didn't have to be mature and dependable. Who didn't have to be concerned about protecting their kid sister from strangers in silver trucks. Who could learn hip-hop without worrying about looking foolish. They just had a good time.

I was going to have a good time. This summer, all summer long. Nothing could stop that now.

The hip-hop teacher looked up at me and smiled, but I ducked away before she could invite me in. I walked back to wait for Hayley.

In the back of the ballet class, I checked my dirty-blonde hair in the mirror. I kind of liked the kinked look. It was fresh and different from any of my friends. Maybe a little freer. *My new style.*

We walked home, and as we approached our house, I saw the silver truck speeding away again. *Now* I was getting a little freaked out. Who *was* that?

"Was that truck at our house?" Hayley asked.

I nodded. "I think so." The door was still locked, so Hayley and I went in. And the dog wasn't barking.

"Why don't you sit down and do your home-work?" I wished my mom would come home soon. Some days I hated being the "adult" around here.

My phone rang. "Sarah!" I flipped it open.

"You made it!" she said. "I just knew you would. Now it would only be too perfect if we got to work together. I'm going to find out if it's possible to request you as a teammate. Why not!"

"I can't wait; it's going to be so fun."

"You'll love it! Even though it's my first year, I know some of the other counselors from church. It's the job everyone dreams of having when they get a little older. If you can come to church with me a couple of times this month and next, you'll meet some of the others. Then they always have a week-end party and hangout training session in May for everyone, the ones from our church and all the oth-ers. It'll be so fun."

"Totally!" I peeked out the window again but saw nothing. "Oh, hey, listen to this weirdness." I told her about the silver truck. "Do you think I'm imagining something?"

"It is strange," she said. "Be sure to tell your mom when she gets home. Okay?"

"Okay."

Her mother called her to dinner in the background. "I gotta go, my mom has dinner ready."

"Okay," I sighed. "See you later." Her mom worked, too, but was always home by four. Unlike my mother.

Just then I heard the garage door opening. Mom!

"Hey there." She swooshed into the room in a light cloud of perfume. "How are my best girls today?"

Hayley, still at the table doing her homework, started hacking. "I've got this cough, and I don't know where it came from." Mom set down her briefcase and purse, ruffled Hayley's hair, and gave me a quick hug and a wink.

"I'll give you a little cough drop after dinner," she said. "That's sure to help."

"Will you read my book to me tonight?"

"Yes." Mom pulled the pot roast from the oven and we sat down at the table.

"Go to bed, girl," I told our Lab, Missy. She curled into a loose oval in her crate, swished her tail one last time, and sighed as she sank into her pillow.

"I was thinking we should pray before eating," I said as my mom and Hayley both held their forks midair.

Mom set her fork down. "Oh, ah, okay." She looked surprised. Hey, I understood. It felt awkward to me, too.

"They do it at Sarah's house," I said. "And Aunt Beth and Uncle Andy pray, too." Hayley nodded her agreement. Mom smiled, tiredly. So I prayed.

"Dear God, thank you for the food. Um, that's all. Amen."

They both looked at me to see if it was okay to eat. I mean, how did I know? I stuck my fork into the pot roast and took a bite. They both followed suit.

"How was your day, Mom?"

"Oh," Mom answered, "good, but hard. If I don't close this account by the beginning of May"—I looked at Hayley, who mouthed the words silently to me at the same time my mother said them aloud—"I'm dead."

I winked at Hayley, and she smiled. My mom always felt she was going to be dead about everything at work. We could even say it aloud while she was still thinking it.

Mom took another bite. "Did you tell Hayley about the camp?"

I nodded. "Yeah, on the way home from ballet."

Hayley looked up and smiled. "I'm *so* excited to be going to camp this summer. I just know I'll meet a fun friend there. I wish you could come, Mommy."

"I'll come for the performance nights," Mom said. Her eyes looked flat and tired, her shoulders slumped. She dabbed her mouth with a napkin and pushed away her plate, still half full. Suddenly she revived. "Let's call Grandpa! He'll be so proud of your very first job offer."

"After dinner, maybe," I said quietly. I noticed she hadn't said, "Let's call your dad." He was hardly ever at home, and I suspected that he didn't pick up when my mom's number showed up on caller ID. They talked less and less as time passed. Oh well. He still sent the check every month.

I mashed a potato over and over with the back of my fork but didn't eat it. I saw my mom open her mouth to say something, but then she closed it, looking disappointed.

Hayley let the dog out to eat her dinner and then began to clear the dishes from the table.

"I'm going to take a bath," Mom announced. "Then I'll help with homework, *and* we'll call Grandpa to brag."

I nodded and went toward my bedroom to get my own homework.

I heard the bath water tumbling into the tub in my mom's bathroom and caught a whiff of her orange aromatherapy candle, so I knew she'd slipped into the water. Just then I heard the doorbell ring. I peeked out of my bedroom window. Through the twilight and mist I could see the silver truck in my driveway. I'd forgotten to tell Mom about it! I couldn't very well let Hayley answer the door. It had to be me.

I peered out of the peephole. It *was* a teenage guy. A cute one, actually. I couldn't see much, but he looked safe. And the water had stopped running in my mom's bathroom, so if I hollered for help she'd hear me.

I opened the door. "Can I help you?"

He was taller and a little older than I was, probably about sixteen. Well, he had to be sixteen in order to drive, but he didn't look much more than a year and a half older than me, so probably no more than that. He ran his hand through his wavy brown hair. "Hi, my name is Jake Cohen. My cousin Davina is marrying your cousin Jed next month."

"Oh," I said. "Would you like to come in?"

He shook his head no.

Hey, wait a minute. "My cousin Jed isn't getting married till the end of June!" I said.

Jake shook his head again. "They changed the date. It's all explained in this, I think." He held out an envelope and a book. A garden book, *Northwest Gardener's Guide*.

I took the envelope and the book. Jake had really blue, dreamy eyes. They crinkled at the corner when he smiled.

Jake explained, "I ran into Jed at the gas station, and he asked if I could deliver these to you and to my sister, Rachel." He must have read the question in my eyes. "Jed was going to bring it to you him-

self, but I offered to do it. New wheels, you know.
Like to drive." He pointed at his truck. "I drove by
a few times—first I wasn't sure if this was the right
address. You know, *Street* versus *Place*. But I finally
figured out it was right."

"Oh, it's very nice of you," I said, then looked at
the book and letter. *What* was in the envelope? I
couldn't open it now—it would be rude.

"Would you like to see my new truck?"

He seemed so earnest and proud. It was still
misting out, so I slipped my flip-flops on and set the
envelope and book down on the ledge by the camp
letter. "Sure, I'd love to see it."

"I worked for a couple of summers to save the
money," he said as we walked toward the truck. "So as
soon as I got my license, my dad took me to buy it."

I pretended not to notice the tiny rust spot on
the back panel. "It's very nice," I offered. "I'm sure
you worked hard for it."

"It *is* sweet," he said. "I'm sorry, you must be getting wet out here," he said when I ran my hand over
my hair.

"Oh no, it's fine," I said. It was kind of him to be
concerned.

"Your hair kind of looks like Maid Marian's," he
said. Then he blushed. "I mean, it's kind of wavy,
since I dragged you out here in the rain."

I smiled. "I like medieval stuff, too," I said.

Jake nodded. "Well, hey, if I can ever be of any help, you know, with whatever Jed sent in the envelope or whatever, give me a holler. I mean, now that I have wheels I can run errands and whatever. I live on Mercer Island, so, you know, it's not too far. I'm glad to help Davina since she's my cousin. And since there were problems the last time . . ."

I opened my mouth to ask what he meant, but Jake blushed again, clearly certain that he had spilled a family secret.

What last time? I hadn't heard anything about that, but I guess that wasn't such a surprise. Jed was my aunt Beth's son, and since my dad had kind of checked out of our lives, we didn't see his side of the family too much anymore.

Jake handed me a slip of paper. "Here's my email address. In case you need anything. About the wedding, or Jed or whatever, I mean."

I tucked it into my pocket. I wasn't supposed to give my email address or phone number to guys without talking about it with Mom. But Jake was practically family, right? Except not *really* family.

"I'll give you mine, too." He handed over the pad of paper he'd pulled out of his tiny glove box. I wrote my phone number and email address down. "CamelotGrrl." Jed smiled and tucked it into his pocket.

He went around to his truck. "You are coming to the wedding, right?"

I nodded. "Wouldn't miss it. Thanks for the delivery."

He smiled and got in, and then I turned and went into my house. I wasn't going to stand there and watch while he drove away, after all. No way!

I walked back into the house and saw the camp confirmation letter sitting there—with its line to sign and the return envelope.

I felt uneasy again.

I shut my eyes, ignored the warning signs, and locked away the troubled bubble in my heart. I clutched the envelope and the *Northwest Gardener's Guide* and started walking toward my room. As I did, I heard my mom on the phone. Already out? Short bath! My mom raced through everything in life, even her relaxing moments.

"Yes, Dad, she's right here," I heard Mom say as she trooped out of her bedroom. "I'm just as proud as can be, as you can imagine."

She handed the phone over to me and mouthed, "Grandpa."

I rolled my eyes and took the phone. "Hi, Gramps."

"How's my little go-getter?" he asked.

"Good, good. I take it Mom told you I got the job."

"She did, and may I say I am not a bit surprised.

How are your grades doing?"

"Fine."

"Glad to hear it. And speech and debate?"

"The season is over, but we won the last meet."

"That's what I like to hear," he said.

"Hey, I meant to ask you. Are you going to church this weekend?" I asked.

There was no answer on the other end.

"Grandpa, are you going to church this weekend?" I repeated.

"Maybe," Gramps said. "I'll let your mom know. Okay?"

"Okay," I said and then said good-bye. I needed to be a regular church attender, according to The Letter. I couldn't just lie. Could I?

"Grandpa is so proud of you." Mom toweled off her hair. "And so am I. I've always been able to count on you, and that means a lot."

I kissed her cheek. She was pink like a shrimp and looked pretty and refreshed, but I noticed she had papers spread out on her bed. "Are you going to read to Hayley?" I asked.

She nodded. "Of course!"

I walked into my room to open the letter from Jed. I wanted to see what was in it before I told Mom it had arrived. Missy followed me into my room. I picked up a dog treat from the little dish on my dresser.

"Missy, sit," I commanded. Missy sat. "Do you think I should have given Jake my email address?" I asked her. Then I waved the dog treat up and down in a vertical line in front of Missy's face. Her head nodded up and down as if she were answering "yes" as her eyes followed the treat up and down.

See? Missy agreed. I tossed the treat to her. She licked my foot and then lay down next to me while I opened the garden book to the middle, where I'd stuck the envelope from Jed.

I pulled out a piece of paper. It had been hurriedly written in scribble.

Hey, Kylie,

I was going to bring this over myself, but I've got a lot to get done in the next few weeks, and since Jake volunteered to take it over, I'm going to save myself some time and just jot it out. I'm going to keep it short because of that, though.

Davina and I are moving up our wedding date because the Empress Hotel in Victoria, where she's always wanted to get married, had an opening for May 7. That changes things quite a bit. I hope you and your family can still come! Anyway, I have a very special wedding day gift for her, but I need a couple of people to help. I thought right away about you and Davina's cousin Rachel, Jake's sister, since I know only close family will be able to make it.

If you're still coming to the wedding and it's okay with your mom, give me a call and I'll fill you in. If not,

give a call anyway and let me know so I can plan some-
thing else. I've missed seeing you guys! I thought maybe
this would be a good way to get both sides of the family
working together. Thanks, Sunshine.

                                                    Jed

I folded up the letter, smiling. I'd forgotten that
he'd called me Sunshine when I was a little kid.
He'd been so good to me. At family parties he'd
always throw me in the pool—so I got some attention—but not too deep, since I didn't like to swim.
He always wanted everyone to like everyone else.
After my parents divorced it'd been kind of weird to
get together with my dad's side of the family. I don't
think my mom felt so good about it, even though
she'd done nothing wrong. She had said we could
go to Jed's wedding in June—when it was going to
be here in town. Was she going to agree to a big,
expensive trip to Victoria, staying overnight, and
being uncomfortable for two days among my dad's
relatives?

And why a garden book? I read the page that I'd
stuck the envelope in. *Love in a Mist*. Dreamy.

I pulled out Jake's email address and tacked it
on my French bulletin board right next to the article
from that morning's paper on teen independence. I
had already conquered a summer job. I was totally
into a new hairstyle. I might even have a shot at a
first love. Would Jake continue to be as interested

in me as he seemed to be tonight?

What kind of problems had happened to Davina?

I *had* to go to that wedding.

I gathered up my courage, smoothed back my Maid Marian hair, and headed toward my mother's bedroom with the *Northwest Gardener's Guide* and Jed's letter in hand.

CHAPTER TWO
rachel's story

Obedient Plant *Physostegia virginiana*
This spiky plant has lovely, tubular purple flowers
with white edging. In good soil it can be a pest, taking over space for other, more desirable plants.

—Northwest Gardener's Guide

*An "Obedient Plant" is also what you
become if you just do what everyone wants year after
year even if it's not really you, just because you don't
want them to stop loving you. You have no personality
then. Just water me. I'm a plant.*

—Rachel Cohen

I was tired of living in the shadow of a dead girl.

I know that might sound harsh, but it was true. Anyone would grow weary of that. What can grow in a shadow? *Rachel, things are going to change, starting now,* I told myself. I sighed. I'd had big words before and always backed down.

I thought about this hard as I dusted around my grandmother's picture frames. Except we didn't call her *Grandmother*. Never! She was *Bubbie*. When I was a girl I used to call it "Bubbie gum," instead of "bubble gum," since Bubbie and bubble sound almost exactly alike. Anyway, Bubbie's crop of photos on the back of her piano was a dust magnet. I took extra time dusting around my parents' wedding photo. There was a picture of me with Jake slipping off the back of a pony. There was a picture of Bubbie and Zayde, my grandfather, who had died since then, both with big straw hats on their last trip to Israel.

Next was a whole collage of Rachel—not *me* Rachel, the *other* Rachel, my dad's sister. Bubbie's daughter. The girl I was named after and couldn't seem to lose though I think I'd been trying for most of my fourteen years. I picked up the collage and stared at it. We had the same dark chocolate eyes—like Dad's, even though Mama's were blue like the irises in Bubbie's garden. Jacob's eyes, too. Rachel had died when she was sixteen, when my dad was twenty, twelve years before I was born.

Bubbie plonked into the room as I set down Rachel's collage. "You're hungry," she informed me. "I made you some cookies." She set a lacy china plate down on the doily on her tea table. She sank into one armchair, I into the other. "You do a good job, Ruchel." She patted my arm as she used my Yiddish name. "You're a good girl. Thank you for coming to help your old Bubbie out with the housework after a hard day at school. You always do what is right."

I chewed both a mouthful of cookie and that thought, too. What she didn't know wouldn't hurt her.

"*My* Rachel, your aunt, she was a good girl, too. She just fell in with those kids who drove too fast, and then there was the accident." Bubbie teared up looking at the collage I'd just dusted. "If only she'd had longer."

I did *not* want Bubbie to get trapped in this holding pattern and never land the plane. "Bubbie," I said gently, "do you want me to clean out that hall closet before Jacob comes to get me? I know you can't get in there with your knees like that." I pointed at her swollen legs.

"My knees, my legs," she said. "What's good about growing old, I ask you? It's a terrible thing to grow old. Yes, please, clean out that hall closet. I'll get a garbage bag and we'll look through things together."

Bubbie hobbled out of the room, and I stopped at the piano one last time before heading toward the hall. The centerpiece was a frame with pictures of everyone in the family—Bubbie and Zayde, the other Rachel, my mom and dad and Jacob and me, Uncle Sid and his wife, Aunt Momo, and all of their kids. Except Davina. Even though Davina was Bubbie's oldest grandchild—and used to be her favorite, I think—there wasn't a picture of her anymore. It had been missing so long I wasn't sure there ever would be a picture of her in there again.

I opened the walk-in closet door and waded in. I cleared aside a forest of heavy coats and leaf-like mittens dangling from hangers. I knew Bubbie rarely wore the stuff, but she kept it for sentimental purposes. I moved them to the back and moved the lighter-weight sweaters forward. I arranged her shoes on the shelf and laced up the boots, which were hard for her to lace now with her arthritis. Together we sorted through what she would give away and throw away. Way back on the top shelf I spied something unusual. A clarinet case!

"What is *this*?" I opened it up, lifted out the mahogany instrument, and waved it at her like a baton. It was good quality—I should know. I played the clarinet in band. I planned to quit at the end of this year. Quitting was going to be one of my first steps of independence. My dad wanted me to keep playing, but I felt I needed to make my own mark. I'd been inching toward getting up the nerve to tell him I needed to quit.

"It was your father's," Bubbie said. "I thought it had gone to Goodwill long ago."

"Daddy played the clarinet?" I gasped. This was

news to me. I'd had no idea he had played clarinet. "Was he any good?"

Bubbie waved her hand. "Yes, yes, of course. Yitzhak is good at everything. He has the golden touch, *nu*? Look at *his* family—you, Yakov, perfect. But who has time for clarinet, I ask you, if you're working hard to save money for college? Not a middle class family like ours, I'll tell you that much. Your father needed to work and save for college, and he did. And where is he now? I'll tell you. He's a successful businessman who can easily provide for his family. No thanks to a clarinet." Bubbie finished with another flourish of her hand. "Off to Goodwill."

I sat there thinking. I sighed. I had caught the slight jab at my Uncle Sid—Davina's dad—and his family. Uncle Sid didn't make the kind of money my dad did. But he was happy. And then, of course, Bubbie blamed him somewhat for Davina's choice. Why, I didn't know.

"Bubbie, how about if I keep the clarinet? I mean, for me to play. You *do* remember I play, right?" She was getting on in years. And I was her youngest grandchild.

"Do I know? How many band concerts have I sat through? Many." Bubbie kissed my cheeks one at a time, her salt-and-pepper bun of thinning hair shaking as she did, a faint mustache feathering her upper lip. "Keep it."

I kissed her back, softly, with great affection. Then I

closed up the clarinet case and set it by my shoes in front of the door.

Bubbie and I sat waiting for Jake and drained our mint tea. Bubbie was unusually quiet, so I picked up the newspaper and turned to work the crossword puzzle next to the comics. An article and list on the opposite page caught my eye. "Teens Need Independence and Excitement." *Oy*. No kidding.

A new and unusual hairstyle. I wish.

A summer job. It was already in the works. Even if my mom and dad didn't know.

A first love. Right. Guys did *not* go for me. They went for skinny blondes. Next!

Something important to believe in. What *did* I believe in, anyway? It bugged me. I had no answer. I pretty much did what everyone told me to do. Who was I?

The doorbell rang. "Yakov is here," Bubbie announced. We got up together, and Jake let Bubbie kiss both of his cheeks before practically shoving me toward the door.

"We gotta go," Jake urged. "Mom has dinner almost ready."

"All right, all right," I said. I slipped my low-heeled sneakers on, grabbed the clarinet case, and headed toward the door. "See you next week," I said to Bubbie. She tried to press a twenty-dollar bill into my hand but I refused. I'd never let her know how much I really hated cleaning.

"Bubbie, I do this because I love you," I said. "Not for the money."

Besides, soon enough I should have money of my own, if all went according to my unrevealed plans.

It was starting to mist on the windshield of Jake's silver truck as we drove the few miles from Bubbie's house to our own. When Jake pulled into the driveway, I leaped out of the car.

"Wait!" Jake called after me. "I have something for you!" But I was already dashing toward the house. There wasn't enough room in the garage for his new truck, so he had to park outside. I didn't want my hair to get wet. I was planning to go to Melissa's house tonight after dinner, and I didn't want it to frizz up.

I ran into the house and deposited the clarinet case behind my bedroom door. I'd figure out what to do with it later. Give it to Dad? Say nothing? I hadn't decided.

"Dinner!" my mother called down the hall after me. I wanted to change from the grungies I had worn for cleaning at Bubbie's and get ready to go to Melissa's. Jake had said he'd drive me if I gave him a buck for gas.

I pulled a shortish skirt out of my bottom drawer, put on a fresh shirt, and pulled my hair into a French updo with little tweaks and tendrils of hair sticking out here and there. I slicked on some lip gloss and text messaged Ellen. *c u soon.*

"Hi." My mom gave me a hug and I hugged her back. I could hear my dad finishing up a phone call in the other room. I poured water into the ruby red glasses my mom set out, the ones that matched her dishes. I loved that my mom always set a nice table. Our house was a home.

Jake sat down before the rest of us and put his napkin on his lap. I sat down next and then Dad came in.

"So where is Mr. In-a-Hurry going after dinner?" Mom set a steaming platter of ravioli smothered with Alfredo sauce on the table. Dad tossed the green salad and portioned some onto each of our plates.

"I have a delivery to make." Jake helped himself to a Jurassic portion of ravioli.

"A delivery?" Dad asked Jake but eyed my hairdo. I hoped the topic would distract him from further inquiry.

"Yeah. For Jed. I saw him at the gas station this afternoon."

"Jed?" Mom asked. "We know a Jed?"

"You know, the guy Davina is marrying. I remembered his car from their engagement party. You know, the red pinstripes, the megabucks tires . . ."

"Oh, *Jed,*" Mom said. "Yes, that's right. Imagine running into him here on Mercer Island." Jed didn't live near us—he lived farther out in the country, whereas we lived close in to Seattle.

"There's only one gas station," I reminded my mother. "It's in the middle of town. And Jake doesn't need an excuse to drive anywhere these days. Hey!" I continued. "You can't make any deliveries till you drop me off at Melissa's house."

"Melissa's house?" Dad interrupted. "Now, I don't know—"

I rushed in with extreme and forced interest before my dad could continue on about Melissa. "So, tell us, Jake, what *is* the delivery?"

Jake stuffed another pasta pillow into his mouth, chewed, and swallowed before answering. "I don't know. It's a big secret. But there's one for you, too," he said. "That's why he was on the Island. He was on his way to our house to bring it to you."

Now everyone was riveted. Silent. Jake looked up. "Want me to go and get it?"

"Yeah!" I said.

I bit into a tomato, then nervously twirled a dressed piece of lettuce on my fork. What could Davina's *Christian* fiancé want from *me*?

Jake pushed back from the table and went out to his truck. A minute later he came back in. He handed over a new *Northwest Gardener's Guide* book and an ivory envelope. "I tried to bring one over to Jed's cousin earlier, but no one was home and I didn't want to leave it in the rain. That's why I have to go back."

I looked at the book. A gardening book? Odd. "Should I open the envelope?" I asked. "Or wait till after dinner?"

"Open it now," my mother said. "The suspense is killing me!" Even my dad stopped eating while I read the note out loud.

Dear Miss Cohen,

I'm Jed Apprich, Davina's fiancé, in case you for-got. I am sure you already know that we heard from the Empress Hotel in Victoria that they have an opening on May 7. So we've moved the wedding up. I have a very special wedding day surprise for Davina but need some help. I would like it if you and my cousin Kylie would help with this. If you're still going to be able to attend the wedding, please give me a call and I will explain it all to you, and to your mom. It would be nice if the families could work together. Thanks again.

Your soon-to-be cousin,
Jed

"A wedding day surprise," my dad snorted. "I'm sure."

Even my mom stared at him. Normally my dad was the kindest person in the world—a *mensch*—someone who was never angry or sarcastic.

"Isaac, whatever do you mean?" Mom asked.

"Remember her last Christian fiancé?" Dad asked.

Ah, now I understood. Soon after Davina had turned into a Christian, she had been about to marry a man who then left her. At the altar. On her wedding day with everyone watching. I mean, he just didn't show up. Then, later, he *called* her to tell her it was off. Truly, it was one of the most painful things we'd ever lived through. Almost more than Davina's becoming a Christian. I shivered, remembering the look on my Uncle Sid's face when *that* had happened.

I would *never* ever cause my dad to feel that kind of pain.

"Jed's not like that," Jake said. "In fact, he seems to be going out of his way to make sure we feel comfortable. He told me that they are getting married in a hotel so Davina's Jewish relatives won't feel awkward in a church. And they're going to have a lot of Jewish stuff in the wedding."

"I don't know. Attending a wedding here in town is one thing. Going out of town? Having Rachel help?" My mother shook her head. "I predict trouble."

At that moment I remembered Davina's humiliation as she was left at the altar, and her missing photo at Bubbie's. Davina had suffered enough. I was going to help. I was growing up, and it was time people realized that.

Trouble? Count me in.

"I'd better make that other delivery." Jake jumped up from the table.

"You're not making any delivery till you clear the table," Mom answered.

"I have a real job now, Mom. Can't Rachel clear it?"

"It's not my night," I said. "And I'm getting a job, too."

The room grew deadly quiet. Uh-oh. How did *that* slip out?

"Can I talk with you guys in the living room?" I asked. My mom nodded and gave Jake "the look." He sighed and started clearing the table. I put my arm around my dad and shepherded him into the living room.

"Now," I said, "about the job."

"What job?" Dad asked.

"My summer job."

"You have a summer job?" my mother asked. "This is the first I've heard of it."

"Well, Melissa belongs to the Yacht and Swim Club, and her dad can get all four of us jobs for the summer. Isn't that great?"

"I work hard so you don't have to," Dad said. "You can go to the Jewish Community Center all summer with the rest of your friends and enjoy yourself. You'll have enough time to work when you grow up. Besides, I don't know Melissa, I don't know anyone you'll be running into, and we don't even belong there."

I stood up. "But, Daddy, you let Jacob get a job the summer after eighth grade. So he could save to buy a car. I want a job, too."

My dad smiled. "Okay, I know. You can help Bubbie. You can clean her house, take care of the yard, all that kind of thing. Her yard needs help. It's overgrown, and I can't get out there to do it. Sid would kill everything if he tried—he has a black thumb. She has a hard time keeping up on the housework. She'll pay you. Or I will."

"I don't *want* to work for Bubbie," I said. "I hate cleaning up. I'm just there to help Bubbie. I don't want *you* to pay me. I want a real job!"

"You're young," my dad said. "You don't need a job." He glanced at the picture of the *other* Rachel on the wall. I knew what he was thinking. That she got killed when she was with people from her job. But why did that have to keep affecting *my* life?

I opened my mouth to say something, but my mom gave me a look that said I probably didn't want to go there just then. So I closed it.

"Can I at least go to Melissa's tonight, then?" I asked.

This time I caught my mom giving him a look on my behalf.

"Yes," he said. "Jake will drive you and I'll pick you up. But change that skirt. And no wearing your hair up like that; you're still a young girl and that's a very mature style. There's time enough for that—later."

I went back into my room, took off the skirt, and put on jeans. I took down my hair, brushed it out, and sighed. Doomed to eternal little-girlhood in Dad's eyes.

Jake drove me over to Melissa's. "What do you think they'll do about the wedding?" he asked.

"I don't know. Do you want to go?"

He just shrugged. Well.

We pulled up to Melissa's, and I jumped out of the truck. "Thanks for bringing me over." Then I walked up to the door.

"Hey! It's Raaaachel!" Melissa screeched and let me in. She had new eye shadow on, with a little too much black rimming her lower lids. It looked very . . . well, dramatic, if I was being kind. Or owlish if I wasn't.

Melissa escorted me down to her room, where Ellen

and Carmel were already waiting. Carmel was trying to braid Ellen's hair. Ellen and I had been friends practically since birth, but I'd just met Melissa and Carmel this year.

"Here, let Rachel do it," Carmel said, tossing the comb in my direction. "She's so much better."

I caught the comb teeth side down and headed toward Ellen. I quickly braided her hair in a crown coiled around her head.

"Why don't you ever do anything with your own hair?" Carmel asked. "You're so good at it."

Ellen looked at me out of the corner of her eye. She didn't spill the beans. She knew enough about my dad to know how much he loved me. Even if he always had his hand on the steering wheel of my life.

We plonked into Melissa's rec room. It was huge, and cool, and had great music and a refrigerator loaded with pop, and chick movies to watch on a large TV. It was just fun to hang out there. Melissa brought out some nail polish and decals, and we did pedicures and laughed while we watched TV. Melissa's dad poked his head into the room.

"So, you all ready for making some money this summer?"

Melissa looked at us. "Well. . .?"

"I'm in," Carmel said. "My parents were all for it." She whispered to me, "I'd never get invited to the Yacht Club without Melissa, and *everyone* is going to hang there this summer. It'll be so fun." She squeezed my hand.

"It's okay with my parents, too," Ellen said.

Ellen's parents had said yes! Maybe that would convince my dad. He knew Ellen *and* her family. And Dad liked her.

"Rachel?" Melissa asked. "How about you? My dad is going to let them know if we're on board or not tomorrow. Otherwise they'll find other people for the job."

"What is the job, exactly?" I asked. "I'm sorry I wasn't here after school when you guys talked about it."

"No problem at all," Melissa's dad answered. "You'll rotate in picking up and cleaning the women's locker room. I know it's not glamorous, but it pays well and you can get into all the club activities all summer. The boating, the parties, the swimming, the campfires."

I felt the weight of the silence. They were waiting for my answer. My dad hadn't *actually, explicitly* said no. Now was my chance to not back off for once and be my own person. "Yes, that's great," I said. "I'm in."

"All right! I'll sign you up tomorrow and they'll close out those jobs. The first training is in a couple of weeks." Melissa's dad left the room.

"Let's get a pop," Ellen said. She pulled me by the hand and walked over to the fridge. "Are you okay with this? Do you not want to go?" She spoke in a low voice.

"No, no," I said. "I really want the job." I snapped open my can, a light spray misting my hand.

"The parties sound good," she said. "Everyone there is really nice, the kids, the adults. The pool is awesome, and there's a sandy beach. I went a few times with Melissa last year."

Ellen had met Melissa in drama club last year, and they'd hung out a bit in the summer, too, before I'd met Melissa. Those were the days I'd sat at the JCC by myself.

Well, there were lots of kids there, of course. Just not my friends. That is really all that counts.

"Come on, you guys, we're waiting on you to start the movie!" Carmel called us back over.

We hung out and had a good time. When Dad came to pick me up right at ten, I wished that Melissa's dad had answered the door so Dad could meet him, because he was a really nice guy, but Melissa got there first—with her owl eyes—and hollered for me.

"Thanks for everything," I said, willing her to keep quiet about the job.

"No problem." We gave a four-person group hug, and my dad held the door open for me.

I flipped the mirror down in the car. "My face looks like a poppy seed muffin!" I counted at least five blackheads on my chin when I pulled the skin tight.

Dad wisely said nothing.

"So what do you think about the wedding?" I asked him.

"I don't know, sweetheart."

"Daddy, will Bubbie come? Is she mad because Davina is marrying a Christian? I mean, it's not like we go to temple every week, just on holidays. You know?"

He shook his head. "Yes, but when Davina stopped being a Jewish person and became a Christian, Bubbie felt abandoned and betrayed. I don't think it's so much that Davina is marrying a Christian, which Bubbie would have been unhappy about but lived with. It's that Davina now *is* a Christian. And even though we aren't really religious, that feels like she's turning her back on her people and her history."

"Is that why Bubbie took Davina's picture out of the frame and never put one back in?"

Dad looked at me. "Really? She did that?"

"Really," I said. "I don't know why."

"Why don't you ask her?" Dad suggested.

"I did, actually," I said, proud of my bravery. "She said it had been water damaged and she needed to get a new one. But, Dad, that was like a year ago."

We drove through the mist toward our house. "I'd like to go to the wedding, Daddy."

He surprised me. "I would, too. I'm not going to leave my niece without her family on the most important day of her life. And I want to be there for Sid. I have a business convention the week after, so I will have to fly out early the next morning." He turned on his PDA at the red light and made a note, then snapped it shut when the light turned green again.

We walked into the house together. "Can I help with whatever they want me to help with?"

Dad set his hat in the hall closet. "You and your mother can call this Jed tomorrow and find out what it is. Then we'll see." He kissed me and then headed into his office to work again, I was sure. He had circles under his eyes, but this was a busy time of year with the interest rates so low, and he didn't want to let any of his clients down.

I kissed my mom good-night, quietly, as she was dozing on the couch in front of the TV. Then I went into my own room and closed the door. I pulled the clarinet out of its red velvet-lined case and closed my eyes, imagining my dad playing it as a young man. There was no reed, of course. It would have gone brittle long ago. I went to pull a reed out of my own case, but then someone knocked at my door. It was Jake.

"What's up?" I asked. Jake didn't usually make late-night chat visits with his sister. "You're home early."

"I'm working in the morning," he said. "Hey, I was just wondering, do you think you want to go to that wedding? To help out?"

Now my radar was up. Why the enthusiasm? I wasn't tipping my hand. "Why?"

"Oh, just wondering. I'd really like to go. I thought if we worked together on it, maybe we could convince Mom and Dad."

I wasn't going to tell him Dad was going and I wanted to help without getting something from him. "So why do you want to go so bad all of a sudden? On the way to Melissa's you couldn't care less."

"Oh, you know. For Davina."

Uh-huh.

"I'll tell you what," I said. "You promise to drive me ten times to wherever and from wherever I want with no questions asked and no gas money, and I'll tell Mom and Dad I think it's important we go."

"Deal." He stuck out his hand so fast I thought he might accidentally hit me.

I shook it.

Now, what was going on *here*?

CHAPTER THREE
kylie's story

Butter and Eggs *Linaria vulgaris*
A hardy plant with soft yellow flowers that has escaped into the wild to become a permanent resident. It is able to grow in tough, rocky, poor soil.
                              —Northwest Gardener's Guide

If you make breakfast for your kid sister every Saturday, and she's sick of cereal, you make toast with "Butter and Eggs" even though you don't really want to cook anymore. But summer is coming. . . .
                              —Kylie Peterson

"Mom is meeting with someone strange this morning." Hayley dipped a corner of her toast into the runny center of her poached egg. "I heard her talking on the phone."

"What do you mean?" I ran the water in the pan and tried to peel out the tiny scales of egg skin clinging to the poacher. Otherwise it'd just bake on in the dishwasher.

"A tribal headhunter," she pronounced.

Bah. Her overactive imagination was heating up again. She'd been reading too many books about exotic places in social studies. Next thing you know the pirates of the Caribbean would be coming to kidnap us. Mom was at work. But she'd better get home before noon to drive me over to Aunt Beth's house.

Jitters and sparks coursed through me at that thought. I tried to keep busy and ignore it. I'd received the letter about the wedding a week ago. Today Jed would be there to explain his plan to me—and to his fiancée's cousin, who was my age and named Rachel. Since things were kind of weird in our family, I hoped I wouldn't be embarrassed. Like if the other family assumed we were all close and everything. I hadn't seen my aunt Beth in like two years, since my dad's last visit.

I swept the floor and lined up the things I needed to take with me on the ledge by the door.

The gardening book. The letter Jed wrote to me. A pad of paper and a pen, just in case. My sunglasses and a pink baseball cap, because Jed said we were going to be outside and I didn't want my scalp to burn. I assembled a neat little pile and then looked at the letter from the camp. There it was, still parked and idling on the ledge eight days later.

I'd signed it already and should send it in. I wanted that job, and the commitment letter needed to be submitted by next week. I didn't want to do the wrong thing and possibly misrepresent myself, but in my heart I didn't really want to do the right thing, either, if it meant not having a summer job. I just wasn't sure what to think. So I did nothing at all.

"Can I stay at Aunt Beth's with you?" Two Band-Aids criss-crossed Hayley's left cheek. "Can I do whatever you're going to do?"

"No. I don't even know what we're supposed to do. I don't even know if I can do it, because Mom isn't sure we can go to the wedding." In fact, she'd kind of hinted to me that we wouldn't go because of the expense and, I think, the weirdness of being there with my dad's family.

Just before noon Mom drove into the garage. "Ready, girls? Come on, Hayley, we're going on a date! Maybe I'll buy some new sheets—since some of mine seem to have shrunk." Hayley grinned, obviously pleased with her successful April Fool's prank.

I grabbed my pile of stuff and my purse and slipped on some flip-flops, making sure that my hair was perfect. My heart raced. Would Jake be there?

"Ready, Mommy!" Hayley tied her shoes up, grabbed her pink powder puff purse, and got into the car. We were off.

Aunt Beth lives about thirty minutes away, out in the foothills of North Bend, where their nursery is located. My uncle is a dentist, but Beth works the fields and provides plants to a lot of city landscapers. They also have a huge blueberry farm, and when we were kids we'd play hide-and-seek in the bushes, snacking on a handful of the fleshy, sweet, quarter-sized berries along the way. Those days seemed so carefree, and so long ago.

The city tapered off into the mountains, and the asphalt softened into green. We were getting closer.

Mom drove up and got out with me. Hayley, too. I scanned the driveway and property. No silver truck. *Piff*.

"Hi, Beth," Mom said as Aunt Beth came out of the house to meet us. She held back a little. I think she wasn't sure whether she'd be welcome or not.

Aunt Beth ran up and hugged her. "Janet, welcome," she said. "I wish so much time didn't go by in between our visits. Nothing like a wedding to bring family together, though!"

Mom beamed. Aunt Beth hugged Hayley, who pointed out her wound at the center of the criss-crossed Band-Aids. "I think it was a poisonous spider that bit me in the night," she said. Aunt Beth smooched the opposite cheek.

Finally Aunt Beth turned toward me and gave me a big hug, then held me at arm's length. Her hands were cracked and her nails short from working the garden, her face more deeply lined than Mom's, for sure. From baking in the sun, I'll bet. What you most noticed about Aunt Beth, though, was the lightness that shone from inside her.

"You are a beautiful young woman," she said, holding my face between her hands. "When Jed told me what he had in mind, I just knew you were the right person. And I'd been dying to spend some time getting together."

My mom shifted on her feet. "Ah, well, I guess Hayley and I will go. Kylie? Call me when you're done and I'll come and get you."

"Are you sure you won't stay?" Aunt Beth said.

"Mom and I are having a date at the mall," Hayley announced.

Aunt Beth laughed. "All right. I understand."

I walked them back to the car, and Mom whispered to me, "Don't commit to anything. I just don't know if there will be enough money for all three of us to go to the wedding. I added it up, and for the weekend and the boat over to Victoria, it will come to around a thousand dollars. I'm not feeling very secure about my job right now, so it might not work. Just hear what he has to say. Okay?"

I nodded but didn't look her in the eye. I knew, too, how uncomfortable she felt being around my dad's family, even though it's not like they were rude or anything.

It's not like it was Mom's fault. But I wanted to go to this wedding!

As Mom and Hayley drove down the driveway, a silver truck drove up. "That must be Jake and Rachel," Aunt Beth announced.

I took a deep breath and smoothed down the front of my jeans.

Jake got out of the truck and opened the door for his sister. What a gentleman! I wondered why she looked so surprised.

They came up toward the front porch, where Aunt Beth and I waited.

"Hi, Kylie," Jake said. "This is my sister, Rachel."

I looked away from him and toward his sister. A slow smile spread over her face. She looked pretty and funny and sweet. I could see the resemblance between the two of them. "Nice to meet you," she said.

"You too," I answered.

Jake stood around but mostly looked at me.

"I'll call you when I'm ready to come home, Jake," Rachel said. "There's nothing for you to do here." She glanced at me. Was she smiling?

Jake looked almost as disappointed as I felt.

Jake took off, and Aunt Beth took us through the house and onto the open-air porch in the back, where she'd prepared some lemonade and a light lunch. "Jed will be right down," she said. Rachel and I sat down on wicker chairs softened with floral pillow pads.

"Are you in eighth grade?" I asked, trying to start a conversation.

She nodded. "You?"

"Yeah." I told her all about my classes and my friends while Aunt Beth hovered in the background. Soon enough Rachel opened up and told me about her school, too. Once we started talking, it was like water gushing from two hoses.

"It's fun to have a job in the wedding, don't you think?" Rachel asked.

"Oh yeah. Speaking of jobs, I hope to have one for this summer. How about you?" I asked her, sipping my lemonade.

"I hope so," she said. Then she looked away.

"I hope so, too," I said. I wanted to tell about Sarah and the camp, but she'd clammed up on the summer job business so I didn't say more. I'd heard the stairs creaking, anyway.

"Hey! Look who it is!" Jed came bounding down from upstairs, almost bumping his head on the ceiling. "It's Santa's little elves."

I got up and hugged him. He smelled spicy and like a fresh T-shirt. "Don't go all goofy in front of Rachel, or her family might not be glad you're marrying into it," I teased.

Rachel coughed and looked uncomfortable again. So did Jed. "Well, that's already a problem," he tried to joke, "but let's not talk about that. Instead, I'll bet you two are wondering what my plan is!"

Rachel and I crowded together, sipping our lemonade and nibbling crackers.

"See, I told Davina that I wanted to take care of the flowers for the wedding. She thought it was a little weird, of course, since I'm a guy. I said since Mom was a gardener it was a part of the wedding we could do. So she said okay, and as you know, we're trying to throw everything together quickly now."

I nodded. That made sense. "So how do we help?"

"Daisies are Davina's favorite flower," Jed said.

"I remember that!" Rachel said. "We always teased her because she loved anything overlooked—stray dogs, kids that were crying, and even the flowers that grew wild and weedy instead of neat little roses or something."

"When we first met last year, we were at a picnic

with friends, and we got to talking and talking and talking. And as we did I wove together a daisy chain for her out of the little daisies growing around our picnic basket, then put it on her head, like a crown. My mom used to do that for us when we were kids."

"Oh," I said. "Totally romantic."

"I can see why she fell for you," Rachel teased.

Jed laughed and nodded. "I think it sparked her interest, anyway. Well, here's the deal. I thought it would be cool to have someone from my family and someone from Davina's family working together. I want the tables and the *chuppah* to be decorated with daisy chains. But I'll be a little, um, busy. So if you two are there, I plan to hire you for the grand sum of a dance each to weave some daisies into chains the morning of the wedding. If we do it sooner they'll wilt. I need four quick hands for several hours in order to make sure that there are enough."

"What's a chuppah?" I asked.

Rachel chimed in. "It's the little canopy that Jewish people are married under."

I looked at her face. It was kind of puzzled.

I was puzzled. "But you're not Jewish," I said to Jed.

"I'm Jewish," Rachel said. "But Davina isn't Jewish anymore."

"Oh yes, she is," Jed laughed. "Davina will

always be Jewish. Even though she now knows that Yeshua, Jesus, is the Messiah. So of course she wants a chuppah!"

If there was one comfort, it was that Rachel looked as confused as I did. How could someone be both Christian and Jewish?

"Are you in?" Jed said.

Rachel nodded. "My mom talked with your mom a little and said it would be okay. I'm in!" She looked at me expectantly. It would be so nice to be a part of this romantic thing. And to get to know her better.

Her brother, too, if I was going to be completely honest.

"Well, I'd love to, but my mom isn't sure if we're coming. The cost . . ." I trailed off.

"If your dad would just come, you could stay with him," Aunt Beth said.

"Is he coming?" I asked, ears perking up.

Aunt Beth sighed. "I don't think so. I put a call in to him. He said he'd think about it, but he had several deals closing that week."

He wouldn't be there. I knew it. I knew by the look on Aunt Beth's face that she knew it, too.

"Hey! You can stay with Leeann in our suite," Aunt Beth said suddenly. "No expense at all except the boat trip from Seattle to Victoria and perhaps a couple small meals. Real cousin fun! I'll talk with your mom."

Leeann was my college-aged cousin. Excitement flooded inside. "I think that will be okay, then." Hopefully I wouldn't have to baby-sit Hayley that weekend. No. I just wasn't going to.

"Is that it for the flowers, then?" Rachel asked, trying to get us back on the topic at hand.

"I've got an extra special surprise for her for the opening moment of the ceremony," Jed said. "And I'll take care of that." He looked at his mother, who looked surprised. "Even my mom doesn't know about that. But you girls can pick out flowers to fill the little glass bowls at the center of the tables, okay? And maybe help with the bouquets. That's why my mom sent along those *Northwest Gardener's Guides*. Use them if you like; thumb through them or come up with ideas on your own. If you can get together and plan those a time or two in the next month and then let Mom know what you choose, she'll order them from a friend in Victoria to be delivered on the day of the wedding."

Rachel looked at me, eyes gleaming. I giggled back. It would be *so* fun. I *had* to be able to go!

"Why don't you practice with the daisies I've set on the porch," Aunt Beth said. "I thought you might like to try weaving some chains while I'm here to help, in case you have trouble. Then your mother—

and brother—can come back in an hour and pick you up."

What a great day!

Rachel and I walked to the end of the porch, where a large wicker swing hung from the ceiling. We both climbed on and set the bucket of daisies between us. Aunt Beth showed us how to slit the stem and feed the next flower's stem through before tying off and making a chain. After a minute or two we got it down.

"So you're Jewish," I said.

She nodded. "My whole family is. Except Davina, of course. Well, I mean, that's what I thought."

"Is that why Jed said your family isn't really happy about the wedding?"

Rachel nodded again. "Because my cousin Davina's become a Christian. I don't know what he means, really, that she can be both a Christian and a Jewish person."

"That confused me, too," I admitted.

"Is your mom your Aunt Beth's sister?" Rachel asked, slipping one daisy stem through the slit made in another.

"No, she's my dad's sister."

"Oh. It's too bad your dad can't come for the wedding."

"Yeah. I guess he's really busy selling real estate in California. Hollywood, you know. It never lets up."

Rachel softened her look and nodded. "I'm worried that my grandmother won't come to the wedding, either. But it's important that we all do. Especially after what happened last time."

A breeze blew onto the porch and through her hair before reaching mine. "What happened last time? I mean, there *was* a last time?" I recalled what Jake had let slip. I needed to know!

"Yeah." Rachel looked at me and then apparently decided to plunge ahead. "Well, Davina was going to be married another time, but the Christian, I mean the guy, left her standing at the altar."

"Oh no! This time everything has to go perfectly, then." I wove the daisies exactly as Aunt Beth had shown us. Rachel was trying something new.

She nodded. "Yes, it does. So even though people aren't happy about the Christian thing, they love Davina so they'll come. Except maybe Bubbie." Rachel seemed to be talking more to herself than to me. I didn't interrupt her thoughts. "I think Davina used to be her favorite. Now maybe I am."

I slipped another daisy into the small chain I was weaving. I wasn't anyone's favorite, really.

"Is your family religious?" Rachel snapped back into reality and turned the conversation toward me. She sipped her lemonade and set it down on the small table next to our swing.

"Um, I guess my Aunt Beth and her family are.

Jed is. But we're *all* Christians," I insisted just a bit too strongly.

"Of course," Rachel said.

"Is *your* family religious?" I asked back.

She shook her head. "Not really. But we're *all* good Jewish people," she insisted right back.

"Of course," I answered.

"You don't think Jed would leave Davina for any reason, do you?"

"No way," I said. "Never." I sat there quietly. But then I realized that I hadn't really ever thought my dad would leave us, either.

Just then Aunt Beth came out onto the porch again.

"Well, you girls get together and decide on the centerpieces. Then let me know what kind of flowers you'd like—just a few kinds, okay, because we're trying to keep the costs down. Davina and Jed are paying for the wedding mostly by themselves. With a little help from friends." She winked at us.

She stepped off of the porch and started weeding. "I've got so many plant orders coming up I should get to work. With business so busy and Leeann studying in Canada instead of helping me, my *own* garden can be a bit neglected."

"What's that?" Rachel pointed to a large plant that was growing but was one of the few in the area with no blooms or blossoms yet.

"That's a special kind of daisy, coincidentally. It's called a Rudbeckia. Black-eyed Susan. Each plant has a botanical, usually Latin name, like *Rudbeckia,* and then a common-use one, too, like Black-eyed Susan."

Aunt Beth took Rachel's garden book from the side of the porch and looked it up and showed her. "It should be a special plant to you, black-eyed Rachel," she teased. Rachel's eyes were true, dark brown. Nearly black. I watched as Rachel blushed with pleasure.

"How come there are no flowers on it?" Rachel asked. I leaned over to look, too.

"There will be. See?" Aunt Beth pointed out a firecracker of tiny fists all over the plant, tightly clenched. "They're waiting for the sun to shine on them. Then they uncurl one by one." She unfolded the fingers from her own hand. "Like this."

"Sweet," Rachel said. "I wish I knew more about plants—taking care of them, which ones grow with other ones. How to build a garden and stuff like that. I seem to kill almost everything I try to grow. Like my uncle Sid."

I smiled at her. "Me too!"

"Bah," Aunt Beth said. "Anyone can learn with time and desire."

Rachel and I sat, still weaving slowly. How would we ever get fast enough to make a ring for every table and the bridal canopy?

And would my mom even let me *go*?

Aunt Beth went into her potting shed and dug out a pot and a trowel. Then she started digging up the Black-eyed Susan.

What is she doing?

She carefully lifted it out of the ground and set it into the pot with some fresh soil. She handed it to Rachel, who took it, gently, from Aunt Beth's hands.

"What do I do with it?"

"Plant it in the sun. The more sun it gets, the faster it will bloom and the more flowers will grow. And water it often, too, black-eyed Rachel."

Rachel beamed and set it next to her. Then she looked over at me just sitting there kicking my feet. "Here. You need a souvenir, too." She joined her tiny daisy chain and mine into a circlet and set it on my head. "You look so pretty. Like a medieval girl, almost."

I had to smile then. "From Robin Hood, maybe?"

"Yes, that's just it!" She laughed. "It's dramatic. I like drama. In fact, I hope to quit clarinet and join the drama club next year."

We nattered on about drama and speech and debate and music and guys—but *not* Jake—and became just as close as the daisies we wove in no time at all.

We made plans to get together in a couple of weeks and email in between about the plans for the wedding flowers. The wedding itself was only four weeks away.

She called her brother and I tried to call my mom, but I had let my cell phone battery get run down. I was trying to juggle too many things, I think. I almost never overlooked a detail. "Can I use your phone to call my mom?"

"Sure." Rachel grinned. "For once I have mine charged up."

I dialed my mom, and she said she'd be right over. Not before Jake had come to get Rachel, I hoped.

Jake pulled up first. Yahoo! He got out and I noticed he looked at me first. "Nice wreath," he said, pointing to my head and smiling. I blushed.

"Hey, I'm the one you're driving home," Rachel teased.

I blushed more deeply. *Drat this fair skin.*

Jake took his cap off of his head, hit her with it, and then put it back on. He carefully lifted Rachel's pot into the back of his truck. When he came back over, he had something in his hand. "I thought you might not have seen this yet," he said. He handed a book over to me. It was about Maid Marian. "It's pretty new," he said. "I just discovered it."

"I'd love to read it. I'll give it back to you at the wedding."

"Or before," he said.

"Okay, we'd better get going. I'm so glad we'll be working together," Rachel said, giving me a hug. "We'll help make it the best wedding ever."

I hugged her back. She was so . . . free. So spontaneous. Not worried. I wanted to be more like that. I was glad she was my new friend. "I'll call you after I talk with my mom, and we'll set up a day to get together."

She and Jake drove off, and I helped Aunt Beth pick up the lemonade stuff while I told her about my summer job. It was so *nice* to be in a family again!

"Camp Moriah? That's a Christian camp!" Aunt Beth seemed surprised.

"Yes, it is."

"Well, I just didn't know you were a Christian now," she said. "I'm so glad to hear it." She hugged me, and I felt myself go stiff in spite of myself.

A Christian *now*? Oh no. There really *was* more to this.

I heard a car pull into the driveway.

"My mom." I headed for the door.

I got to the car as my mom got out. I reached into the open backseat window and set my crown on Hayley's head; she squealed in delight. "It's yours, though," she said.

"I'll get another one someday." I was going to the wedding, and Hayley probably wasn't. She might as well have something fun and pretty.

My mom and Aunt Beth talked for a few more minutes, and then Aunt Beth gave me a warm hug. "We'll see you soon, kiddo," she said and winked. "Glad to hear about that summer job."

My mom beamed. "We're just so proud."

Once we were on our way, Mom said, "Aunt Beth mentioned you staying in the suite, and I think that will be just fine. Do you understand that I can't go?" she asked. "But we'll go to the party in June that they'll have for everyone who can't make the wedding."

All at once I felt like floating. I was going! I nodded. "Thanks so much for letting me go, Mom." I told her all about the flower plan. Even Hayley thought it was dreamy. We got home about half an hour later, and I went into my room, shut the door, and flopped down on my bed to read *Maid Marian*.

An hour and six chapters later I walked out to scrounge for a snack. "Oh, hey, Sarah called on the home phone," Mom said. "She tried calling on your phone but got an immediate message."

"Yeah, I let the cell battery run out. I'm sorry. Great! I'll call her back."

"Oh, no need. I took care of it."

My face chilled. "You took care of it?"

"She called to see if we wanted to go to church with them tomorrow. Since Grandpa already told me he wasn't going, I thought you'd enjoy that. So I said I thought we'd like to go."

Mom hummed as she threaded chunks of marinated chicken onto skewers for barbecuing. "Her mom thought that we might like to come once and meet the people in charge of the camp staff. I said that was a great idea. We're going to meet Sarah's family at the church a little before nine."

Oh no. What would they say? What if they asked where *we* went to church? What if they asked my mom something churchy, about which she knew nothing, or if she didn't know the words to any music and it was *so* obvious? "I don't think that's necessary. I mean, you can meet them another time, right? You're probably tired. You've been working hard all week."

My mom stopped what she was doing. "Don't you *want* us to go?" She looked hurt. "This whole church thing is important to you now. I want to meet the people you'll be working with several hours every day, and the people in charge of where Hayley will be this summer." She pushed her hair behind her ears with her clean hand.

I sighed. What could I say? "Okay. But, um,

since we're new and all, maybe it would be better if we didn't talk too much. You know? Not ask too many questions or talk too much about our own church."

"What church?" Mom asked.

"You know, Gramps' church. Our church."

"Oh. Okay, fine." Mom looked confused. Now if only Hayley would keep quiet. I didn't want anyone to spill the beans.

Spill what *beans, Kylie?* came a pressing question inside my own head.

—

The next morning I was up at like seven o'clock. I had suddenly remembered that Sarah always brought a Bible to her church, and I think her parents did, too.

I ran through the living room and looked under the bench in the front room. I thought we had a Bible in there, but I wasn't sure. I had found it one Saturday morning a few months ago and had paged through it for an hour, absorbed, while Mom worked and Hayley watched TV.

I dug through the bench again. Yep, it was the

New Testament. That was the same as the Bible, I was pretty sure. I don't even know where it came from. It was tiny, not like Sarah's, but it would do.

I breathed easy, went into the bathroom, and started to unwind my braids, then shook them out. An hour later I was ready to go. "Do I look okay, girl?" I asked Missy. I held a dog biscuit in front of her, waving it up and down. She bobbed her head in agreement.

"Thanks!" I tossed the treat to her and we were both happy.

I softened with tenderness when Hayley arrived out of her bedroom door. No sling, no Band-Aids, no inhaler. She'd put on a pretty dress, just a little too short because we hardly ever wore dresses. She'd tugged her hair back into one long pony and put a band around it.

"You look beautiful, Hayley," I said.

She beamed. "Thanks."

My mom looked pretty, too. "I'm kind of looking forward to this," she said. I peeked into her bedroom. Half of her bed was covered with work papers and an open briefcase. She'd probably worked late into the night.

We each ate a piece of toast and jelly, and Mom downed two cups of coffee before we made our way into the car. Mom had printed out a map from MapQuest. I hoped it was right. I didn't want

Sarah's family waiting there for us.

Once in the car I drilled them again. "No talking about church. Okay? No saying how often we go, or noticing stuff that's totally different."

"Why are you telling us what to do?" Hayley asked.

Because I don't want to mess up our summer plans, that's why, I felt like saying. "I just want things to go right, that's all."

We pulled into the parking lot and parked, then met Sarah's family by the door.

"Would you like to go to Sunday school?" Sarah's mom asked Hayley as my mom nodded her agreement. "You get candy on your first day, and there are lots of fun games."

Hayley easily agreed.

"C'mon," Sarah said to me.

"Bye, Mom." I hoped it would all be okay.

The middle school class was, like, so cool. *This is church?* I asked myself. A band played, and even though I didn't know the songs, they put the words up on a screen. There was a coffee bar in the back and we both got a latte.

When it was time for the lesson, I pulled my Bible out of my purse. "Cool," Sarah said. "You brought one! Nice and small!"

See? That's why I love her. She never makes fun of anyone and always finds something good to say about everyone. I smiled back at her.

The teachers were a young couple, and they got up and talked about Jesus, how He calls us to come and follow Him. Sometimes we don't know where He's going to take us, like a trusted friend covering our eyes for a surprise party, but that's okay. He just says, "Follow Me." And if we stick close to Him, we always can follow, because we never lose sight.

Strangely, for one who always liked to chart her own path, it all made perfect sense to me. I think I was tired of charting. I closed my eyes. I would love to stick close. Be free. I'd really love that.

Afterward they showed a movie of the camp— kids laughing with sweating Popsicles in hand, slick from climbing out of the mud pit, victorious at the top of the rock wall. Sun. Fun. Lots of people my own age hanging out together. Making s'mores at night. The movie ended and we were dismissed.

Sarah elbowed me. "Hey, there's Ben. He's in charge of the camp staff." She propelled me toward him.

"Hey, this is my friend Kylie. She's going to be on staff with us this year as a junior counselor."

Ben stuck out his hand. "Cool. We're going to have a great time. Training will start in a couple of weeks. The kids will look up to you; you'll be able to teach them a lot." I guess I hadn't really thought about that so much. I felt inspired. I would teach them *good* things!

Sarah and Ben were chatting. "Just a heads-up," Ben said. "At our first training party we all share and get to know one another. You know, hang-out time, but also we'll be sharing our testimonies on Sundays till then, some of us who are at this church. It's really encouraging for each of us to hear how God's working in our lives."

"Okay," I said. I had not a clue what he was talking about. But he sure seemed nice.

"I know you feel like you're a stranger here, but you won't have to say much when it's your turn," Sarah said. "Just tell people a little about when you became a Christian and what you've been up to lately. No pressure." She grinned at me. "And guess what? I worked it so that we're both teaching second grade!"

We met up with my mom and Hayley in the library. Sarah's family didn't look shell-shocked, so I guess everything went okay. We took them to meet Ben on the way out, so my mom would know what was going on with camp.

On the way to the car I got a sinking feeling. *When I became a Christian.* Something about this was very wrong, and it was going to blow up in my face in front of everyone unless I figured it out.

"Well then," Mom said on the way home. "They seemed nice. Oh, and hey! I sent your camp counselor acceptance in yesterday. With everything going on it must have slipped your mind. I wanted to make sure it got in on time. You always help me with the details of *my* life; I wanted to help you, too. Is that okay?"

"Hooray!" Hayley licked the sucker they gave to new visitors, turning her tongue into a purple highway. "We're going to camp!"

I sank into my seat. *She sent my acceptance letter in!*

CHAPTER FOUR
rachel's story

False Heather *Cuphea hyssopifolia*
Small shrub with pretty lavender flowers that resembles true heather in many ways but is not a true heather plant. Once it takes root it grows profusely and can be hard to get rid of, strangling any true heather trying to grow alongside it.

—Northwest Gardener's Guide

I don't know anyone named Heather, but I know about true and false. "False Rachel" is blooming in a lot of places I don't want her to—taking hold, hard to get rid of. I am going to have to yank her out by the roots if I want to see "True Rachel." You know . . .

—Rachel Cohen

"So Ellen's dad is going to pick you up and take you to the Yacht and Swim Club?" My dad folded back the newspaper and finished up his orange juice.

"Yeah. And you're going to pick me up this afternoon?"

He nodded. "If I said I'll be there, I will. You can trust your old dad. Put your clarinet in the trunk of the car; I'll take you to your clarinet lesson right after I pick you up. Ellen doesn't need a ride home?"

I shook my head no.

"I'm going to a meeting till two. Then tonight we'll catch a movie with Mom and Jake. Okay?"

I nodded and smiled. I had a surprise for him this afternoon. I'd arranged it earlier this week.

I checked my watch and decided there was enough time to water my plant before going. It was sunny today. Maybe it'd bloom soon.

I'd kept the Black-eyed "Rachel" daisy in the pot it came in. It made it easier to move to a sunny location. I carried it down the sidewalk and set it where it would get sun all day. After dribbling some water around the base of the roots—like Kylie's aunt Beth had shown me—I left it on the side of the driveway. I'd bring it back in tonight.

I couldn't wait till it bloomed. But what if I killed it? A gardener I'm not. But I'd like to be! I wouldn't mind trimming Bubbie's overgrown yard, even. If someone else would do the cleaning.

I checked my watch and ran inside. Where was my bathing suit? I wished my mom would stop cleaning my room. I put everything where I wanted it, and she put it where she thought it should go. I finally located my bathing suit and tossed it and some hair stuff into my beach bag. It was only the middle of April, but the Swim Club had an indoor pool, too. It was so cool of Melissa to invite us. I threw a hair claw into my bag. At least my dad didn't object to my hair being twisted in a *claw*.

I grabbed my clarinet—and Dad's—and sneaked them out to the trunk. *Please, God, don't let him look in the trunk before he picks me up.* I slammed the trunk and went to grab a diet pop from the garage fridge.

"Everything's ready!" I hollered.

"What, I'm deaf that you have to scream at the top of your lungs?" Dad walked into the garage, slipped his feet into his loafers, and rubbed his forehead. Must have been a hard week at work. Dad always rubbed his temples when work wasn't going well.

"I didn't know where you were," I said. I opened my can and wriggled the tab loose. Then I dropped the tab into the can.

"I don't want you to choke." Dad gently took the can from me and threw it away. Then he got me a new one from the fridge, wiped off the top, and handed it to me.

I turned my head and rolled my eyes.

Ellen's dad arrived, and I kissed my dad good-bye and hopped in the back of Ellen's SUV. Her dad chatted with mine for just a minute, and then he backed out of the driveway. A few minutes later we arrived at the Yacht and Swim Club.

It was so cool. There was a huge parking lot, and the baskets hanging from the green copper lamp posts already winked with early spring flowers. The parking lots and the driveway had been freshly asphalted—the very color of Melissa's eye liner!

"Can you believe we're going to work here?" Ellen whispered. "I mean, once you're in, you're in. We can work summer after summer and swim and party and whatever!"

Her dad smiled. "We can share carpooling with your mother and dad," he said to me. "You girls should arrange that."

I nodded weakly and didn't answer. He caught my eye for a minute but I looked away. Was he still golfing regularly with my dad? Maybe I should pray for rain for a few weeks till this was all straightened out and Dad understood my point of view. But then I got brave. Didn't that newspaper article say that teens *needed* a summer job? And wasn't I a teen? There you go.

We walked inside and checked in at the front desk. Melissa had left guest passes for us, and we followed the yellow floor arrows to the back.

"Are they meeting us in the locker rooms?" I asked.

"I think the training is first. Remember? This week is the first training class for our job. It's our first job! Did you bring your social security number?"

"Oh," I said. "I—I didn't know this was a training class. This is the first day on the job?"

"Kind of," Ellen said. "Rachel—what's up? You look like you're trying to digest thumbtacks."

I sighed. "Come into the locker room."

We stuffed our swim bags into a locker, and I sat on a polished bench with her. "Well, it's like this. My dad doesn't know I took the job yet."

Ellen's eyes opened wide. "Why not?"

"Let's just say it's going to take a little bit of time to warm him up to the idea."

"So he doesn't know you're working today?"

"*I* didn't know I was working today. I thought it was a hang-out fun time. Maybe a tour. I don't know. I've had a lot on my mind with my cousin's wedding and school and all."

Ellen nodded. "What are you going to do?"

My dad was at a meeting. Jake was at work. My mother was at a Jewish Community Center meeting planning the Matzo Brie Brunch for Passover next week. "I don't know. I guess I'll make the best of it. I mean, I'll sit here and learn the training and see how good it's going to be, and then I'll really be able to tell him how safe it will be. He's going to have to learn to trust me."

Ellen sat quietly. "You know, if you want me to skip the job this summer and just go to the JCC with you, I will."

I reached over and hugged her. "If I had to pick any best friend in the world, it would be you. You're the best. But no, it's all going to be okay. I need to make a stand. And this is it."

Ellen locked her pinky with mine like we did in second grade. I smiled at the memory. "Then let's go have fun, okay?"

"Okay," I smiled. Then I twisted my hair up in a claw and pulled just a few tendrils out. New hairstyle number one, I thought, remembering the newspaper article at Bubbie's.

Melissa and Carmel were saving seats for us in the training room. There was a whole raft of cute guys—and very few blondes. Maybe I'd have a chance for the first love the newspaper article talked about!

We parked in neat rows of chairs in a meeting room trying to check everyone out without looking obvious. The woman in charge got up and outlined the various summer jobs. Then she separated us into groups— those who would be working the snack bar, lifeguards, front desk, and finally, the lowest on the food chain, locker room cleaners.

"Sorry that we're the bottom-feeders," Melissa whispered. "It's our first year on the job, so we have to take the worst jobs. Next year it's snack bar for us. Outside on the sand, in the sun." We reached our hands into the middle, one on another, as a show of solidarity.

Once we were divided into groups, our group leader

gave us name tags. "Hi, I'm Joanie, and I'll be your boss but really your friend." She had a welcoming smile. "Let's go over what your jobs will be. It's easy, you know."

And it *was* easy. Wiping stuff down, mopping the floor when it got too wet, making sure the towel cans were brought to the laundry room regularly. The club provided towels—100 percent Egyptian cotton. My mom would be impressed. For a few hours a day of work we could come to any event the Yacht Club held, and we could swim any time. We could even have guest passes. I read the summer fun list posted in the locker room on the teen board.

- Weekly Bonfires—we supply the marshmallows and chocolate, you supply your voice and sense of fun!
- Pontoon Parties—What Floats Your Boat? Come and find out. Anyone aged 13–17 welcome.
- Shipwreck Party—Are You Down With It? We are. Sign-ups start Memorial Day. See the front desk.

Ellen, standing next to me, squealed. "Fun, fun, fun—and free!"

I smiled back. Our families weren't hurting by any means, but neither she nor I had the kind of money that would get us into the Yacht Club. Were we Rockefellers? No way. It would be nice to have something special on my own—without Jake—since he had a job he was proud of, at Radio Shack. And I'd have cash!

Joanie arrived with a clipboard. "If you guys can sign

up here, let me know what hours you'll be available, that would be great. We'll need your social security numbers, your family phone number, and your parents' names."

I felt sick. Last boarding call. The Titanic Party was happening right now and I was going down. Why didn't everyone else seem to have this struggle growing up? I was mad at my parents and mad at myself.

I spoke up. "Contact them for what?"

"Oh, you know, if there's an accident or anything."

"In the summer, right?" I persisted. "Not now?"

Melissa and Carmel looked at me, but Ellen looked straight ahead.

"Right," Joanie said. When the clipboard came around, I had to leave my social security number blank. I put down my personal cell phone number, not our home phone. Joanie had written the next training date on the top of the clipboard—one month away, May 14. I had a month to prove myself to my parents before bringing it up. One month to show them how responsible and trustworthy I was.

"Let's go swim for a while!" Melissa said. "They have the slide up, and it's 'all teen' till two."

We went to change. I caught a glimpse of myself in the mirror, the claw holding back my hair, tendrils curling around like pea shoots. I looked at my figure in my bathing suit. Ick. Flat as a matzo, almost. Oh well. Mom said she developed later, too. Why did everyone else in my group have to look like a figure eight?

Hanging in the pool picked up my spirits, though. Hope? False hope? I didn't know. I just felt like I could make it all work out somehow. I had a month. I glanced at the clock. I needed to be in front by two o'clock so that my dad didn't get out of the car. It was important that no one talked about this before I'd had a chance to talk with him about it.

We played ball tag and Marco Polo in the pool. There were lots of both guys and girls, and Melissa knew almost everyone. They were mostly all nice. They passed the ball and encouraged you, and I got picked for a team right away. I'd thought a lot of people here might be snotty, being so rich, but it wasn't that way.

At one-thirty I got out of the pool. "I gotta go—clarinet lessons," I said.

"I thought you were quitting clarinet?" Carmel said.

"I am. But I'm going to finish out the school year."

Melissa nodded. "Good idea."

Then they went back to swim, leaving Ellen and me on our own. I bent down over the pool and hooked pinkies with Ellen, who had swam to the edge. "I'm here to talk about anything you want at any time," she said.

"I know," I said. "I'll deal with it. I will."

"Sooner is better than later. It'll bug you."

"I need to figure out how to do it right," I said.

"Sooner," she said and winked. Then she went back to swim with the others. I went into the locker room, dried off, and got dressed. On a whim, I redid my hair and put it back into the claw. It was my first test into honesty. If Dad didn't like that kind of flip-up, we'd talk about it. Openly.

I got into the car and watched his face. He didn't make any comment on the hairdo, though I noticed he looked at it. I almost dared him to say something. Then it would be out in the open and I wouldn't have to bring it up. I think I'd have preferred that, actually. Instead, he just rubbed his temples and drove on.

"My lesson is a bit longer this time," I said. "Can you come in toward the end?"

Dad looked at me, surprised. Normally he or Mom just waited in the car and read while I went in for the lesson. My teacher's studio was small, and normally it freaked me out to have them listen while I played.

"Sure, sure," he said.

"About quarter after, okay?"

"Quarter after. Fine," Dad said.

We drove up in front of my teacher's house, and Dad put the car in park and popped the trunk from the inside. I got out and grabbed my case—and his—and hid them in front of my body as I made my way to the front door.

I walked into the house, where Mrs. Rosenthal waited for me. Her earlier student had already left. Last week she had been kind enough to move my lesson to the morning so I could meet with Kylie. Since we were going to get together on Saturdays, and since the wedding would be on a Saturday, we'd have to tweak a few more lessons, too.

Her carefully manicured living room, where the lessons took place, was a period piece right out of the seventies. Low couches slung on three sides of the room—you know, those couches they always show in movies with psychiatrists? With people lying on them with their arms thrown over their heads, talking about their problems? A piano stood on a dais, four skinny legs holding up a full rack of keys. Near the dais were two firm chairs for those of us taking woodwind lessons. A swag of light blue silk was smeared across each window in neat little arcs like carefully applied eye shadow. The carpet was well cared for but not new.

"Thanks for agreeing to look at this." I handed over my dad's clarinet.

"Yes, yes, of course," she said. "No lesson next week—first day of *Pesach*—so a little longer this time won't kill anybody." I smiled. She reminded me of Bubbie, using the Hebrew word *Pesach* for Passover. Well, she was Bubbie's friend, after all.

She took my dad's clarinet case from me and opened it up. She sucked her breath in between her teeth. "Oy, what an instrument," she said. "And your Bubbie was going to get rid of *this*?"

"My dad had to quit lessons," I explained. "I think it was kind of painful for her to look back on it."

"Pain makes us do lots of things," Mrs. Rosenthal

agreed. She unscrewed the ligature and slid it off. "I see you polished it up. No gunk underneath it. Good, good."

She ran her hand down the smooth barrel and then slipped a reed into the mouthpiece. "So do you think your dad can still play this?"

I nodded and grinned. "My dad is good at everything."

"After your lesson," she said, "we'll find out."

Excited, I peeked through one of the blue silk draperies; Dad was still in the car, reading through his paperwork. I settled into my chair, set my music on the stand, and played my lesson for the week. Is the clarinet an easy instrument, I ask you? No. Oh, it's easy enough to make it wail like a cat caught in a barn gate, but to make the smooth, understated notes that sound just right takes years of practice. This year I'd learned to transpose music into different keys and to play an alto clarinet as well as a B-flat clarinet. I was first chair in band at school.

If you took band, though, you couldn't be in drama club. I might end up being really good at drama—who would know? And Carmel and Melissa and Ellen were going to be in drama. Staying in band didn't allow me to try anything else. My dad thought drama was a "foolish waste of time," which told me right there I should maybe investigate it.

I finished my piece and set the clarinet down.

Mrs. Rosenthal stared at me for a minute. "Would

you mind playing that once again?" she asked.

Uh-oh. Maybe my mind had wandered. It, um, did that fairly often. I ran through the piece in my mind. I don't think I'd made any mistakes.

"Sure," I said. She moved from her chair, next to mine, to one of the blue silk couches. I started the piece over again. Sometime during the piece I closed my eyes.

At the end I held my instrument up for a minute, then laid it across my lap while Mrs. Rosenthal made her way from the couch to the chair.

Once there, she wiped her eye with a tissue that had been tucked into her pocket. "That was lovely, Ruchel," she said, using the Hebrew form of my name.

"Why did you want me to play it again? Did I make some mistake the first time through?"

"Oh no," she said. "I just wanted to enjoy it a second time as a listener, as an appreciator. Not as a teacher."

I took a deep breath and felt the hurt and joy mix in my heart. It was the nicest thing she'd ever said to me.

We finished my lesson, and then there was a knock at the door. "It's your father."

Daddy waited at the door and Mrs. Rosenthal let him in. "Come, come, Yitzhak," she said. "Your little girl has a surprise for you."

Dad looked surprised as he stepped into the house and respectfully wiped off his shoes on the rug right inside the door. I waited for Daddy, and Mrs. Rosenthal drew the chair she normally sat in closer to the one I was sitting in.

Daddy sat down in the chair as Mrs. Rosenthal handed the old clarinet to me. I handed it over to Daddy.

"What—where?" Dad took the clarinet in his hand. "Why, this is my clarinet. Where did you find it?"

"Bubbie's closet. When I was helping her clean out a few weeks ago. She said you were a great player."

Dad ran his hand over the silver keys, touched them, and watched the pads quietly whisper against the holes in the barrel. He turned it over and looked at the ligature. "There's a fresh reed in here!"

I nodded. "I told Mrs. Rosenthal that my dad is good at anything. I thought you might want to play."

"Oh, oh, no," he said. Then he looked at Mrs. Rosenthal. I knew what he was thinking. Mrs. Rosenthal did, too. He didn't want to play in front of anyone after having been away so long.

"Did you hear that? My oven bell. I'll just get back to my kitchen. If dinner is one minute late, Abe moans and groans like he hasn't eaten all week. Crazy man. Why I keep him after all these years I'll never know." She pottered back to the kitchen.

I hadn't heard a bell.

"Why did you bring it *here*?" Dad asked, turning the clarinet over in his hands.

"I wanted her to look at it and make sure I cleaned

it up good and that it was playable before I gave it back to you."

Dad nodded. "Thorough, just like your old man."

He licked the reed for a minute.

"Why did you quit playing, Dad? Did you hate it?"

He shook his head. "No. Bubbie and Zayde didn't have a lot of money, and when it came time for me to work, I went to work. Zayde thought clarinet was a foolish waste of time. I don't think Bubbie did, but she knew I needed to spend my time preparing for school. So that was that. They got me a job at the hardware store, and I worked."

We were a lot alike in many ways, Daddy and I. He couldn't stand up to Zayde, and I couldn't stand up to Dad.

My dad put his mouth on the clarinet, and guess what came out, after all these years? No stuck-cat sound, huh-uh. No calf moaning. A clear, pure, haunting note that I had yet to achieve.

After a few minutes of warm-up he played a song from the beginning of my book, and then he played the song I had just spent weeks—months, maybe—practicing.

It was wonderful.

"You should play a duet, I tell you." Mrs. Rosenthal came back into the room, wiping her hands on an apron.

"A duet? Oh no. I'm afraid I would have to be your student as well as Ruchel if that was ever going to happen," Daddy teased. "And there's *still* no room for a foolish waste of time. No, we have to depend on Rachel for the clarinet talent from now on, I'm afraid."

"Yes, well, it's too bad that she's quitting clarinet, then. What a shame, what a waste. But there's no telling these kids what to do these days. They do what they want to do." Mrs. Rosenthal set about helping me to pack up my music.

I felt my heart sink into my toes. I felt my dad's eyes on me. I could imagine him rubbing his temples. I finally got the nerve to look up.

Dad set his clarinet down on his lap. The soft jazz father-daughter moment was over, and a sharp tone with wrong notes was back.

"Rachel? Quitting clarinet?"

CHAPTER FIVE
kylie's story

Breath of Heaven *Coleonema pulchellum*
Breath of Heaven has fragrant flowers, tiny pink blooms on a hardy evergreen plant that likes sun. Stalks have a pleasant aroma when crushed.
—Northwest Gardener's Guide

I had no idea that day would bring about a "breath of heaven" in my own life. In fact, it would bring me closer to heaven than I had ever been before, and from that point on there was no turning back.
—Kylie Peterson

"Is it okay if Rachel's brother drives us?" I hollered down the hall. "My chores are done." It was Saturday, just after noon. *Please* let her say yes.

Mom opened her bedroom door and held her hand over the mouthpiece of the phone so the person on the other end couldn't hear her. "How old is he? Is he a good driver?"

"Sixteen and a half. He's driving Rachel, too, so I'm sure he's a good driver."

"What time will you be back?"

"Before five, for sure."

Mom hesitated. "Well, take your phone with you." I felt a little guilty from the start. I knew that Jake was special—not *just* Rachel's brother—but Mom didn't know that. Of course, between the massive work load she brought home every night and her phone conversations behind closed doors with someone whose number I didn't recognize on caller ID, she didn't have much time to figure out what was going on in my life anyway.

Hayley sat in front of the TV, her leg wrapped in a huge Ace bandage, crutch leaning against the La-Z-Boy, coloring pictures of kids at camp in canoes, kids making s'mores.

"Gonna be a good girl, Missy?" I talked to the dog instead. "Obey whatever Hayley tells you to do?" I asked as the dog lazily licked my hand and Hayley's leg. Hayley petted her behind the ears. I grabbed a piece of leftover lunchmeat from Hayley's plate and waved it up and down in front of Missy. Missy nodded yes, of course. "Good dog!"

I heard the doorbell ring.

"Ready?" Rachel had come to the door to get me. Her long hair tumbled over her shoulders and down her back.

"Ready!" I patted my own Maid Marian 'do. We were going to Davina's house, Rachel's cousin, the bride, to quiz her and come up with a game plan for the flowers. Davina didn't know any of the details, of course; that was one of Jed's surprises. She *did* know we were helping with the flowers in some way.

"You can sit up front," Jake said to me, grinning. Rachel popped him a hardball look, and I smiled.

"Thanks, but I think it's better if I sit back with Rachel." I wasn't going to push it *that* far. Yet. I squished in the smallish backseat of the truck and buckled in next to Rachel.

It'd been two weeks since we'd been planning at my aunt Beth's house, but Rachel and I'd emailed back and forth a couple of times.

After about fifteen minutes Jake dropped us off at Davina's house in Bellevue. "I'll be back soon," he said. "Mom will be mad if we're late for the Seder tonight."

Rachel nodded, and we walked to the door of Davina's duplex. A woven welcome mat rested neatly in front of the door, and potted red silk geraniums guarded each side like the red-coated dudes at Buckingham Palace in London.

Rachel hesitantly pushed the doorbell. Within seconds Davina opened the door. Except for her blue eyes she could be Rachel's older sister.

"Welcome!" She enveloped Rachel in a deep hug and then hugged me, too. A lacy apron circled her slender waist; her long hair was twisted back and up.

"I recognize that! That's Aunt Momo's apron," Rachel said, sounding mad, after kissing her cousin's cheek.

I looked at her. I knew she loved Davina. She had told me over and over again how much it meant to her to make sure this wedding went just right. But she definitely looked upset. Maybe something had happened between them since I talked with Rachel last.

"You're right!" Davina said. "It *is* my mom's apron. She always wears it to get ready for Passover, and I am too. Since I'm having Passover here this year, she is letting me use it."

Rachel opened her mouth to say something but then closed it again. I could feel her discomfort. Maybe I'd better change the station.

"We've been emailing about the flowers and stuff," I said. "And I know Jed wants it to be a surprise, but we thought that with you being the bride and all it would be good if you let us know some of the things you'd like."

"How sweet!" Davina laughed. "I have to admit, it's a little strange to turn over the whole flower thing to Jed, my being the bride and all. But I trust him, and I know he must have something unusual planned."

Rachel and I shared a grin.

"Let's sit down at the table here," Davina said. "I had to move the couch up against the wall so I could extend the table for all of my Passover guests tonight. I meant to get this all set up earlier, but I was out late last night."

Her eyes did have circles under them. Well, only two weeks till her wedding. No wonder she was tired.

Davina went into the kitchen and brought back three glasses of a lovely fizzy, fruity drink. Then she sat down with us.

Rachel spoke up. "Kylie brought a notebook; do you want to tell us some of the things you'd like?"

Davina sat down in one of her covered wooden chairs. "Well, I think it'd be nice if there were some daisies involved," she said. I willed myself not to look at Rachel and give away any part of the secret. I could see out of the corner of my eye that she was looking straight ahead, but a tiny dimple in her cheek disclosed a bit of a smile. Davina didn't seem to notice.

"That's about all," she said. "Something pretty to carry to the altar, but not too heavy. I had a friend who took up a twenty-five-pound bouquet and almost passed out before the end of the ceremony."

"Nothing heavy," I promised. I looked around her apartment. What a beautiful, clean sense of style she had. A few paintings on the wall, a small potted plant sleeping in one corner. Her brown sofa had a hand-knit blanket tossed over the back for cozy evenings. In one corner was a used piano.

"Do you play?" I asked, looking at it. There were rows of pictures lining the top.

"I do play some," she said. "Most of our family is musical." She pointed at Rachel. "This little woman is quite a clarinetist."

Rachel frowned and changed the subject really fast. It was kind of weird, I have to admit. Rachel seemed awkward here, even though Davina was her cousin.

"What are those?" Rachel pointed out the flowers in a small glass bubble vase in the center of the partially set table. I looked at the bouquet—like lollipops gathered in a child's hand.

Davina laughed. "We made those in class this week. I taught my kindergartners how flowers drink. We took some white daisies"—she smiled—

"naturally, and cut their stems down. Then I set some in a glass thick with pink food coloring, some in a glass with yellow, with blue, etc. When we were done, we had a bouquet of beautiful flowers and a science lesson sneaked in to boot!"

"I wish you were one of my teachers!" I burst out.

Davina smiled. "And I wish my kindergartners could come to the wedding." She sighed. "That's the one bad thing about this rushed Victoria wedding. It's my dream come true, but I can't take my students. I can tell you something about the flowers that I couldn't tell my students, though."

She rearranged the daisies in their vase. "These have special meaning for me as a believer in Jesus. They remind me that God colors me with His goodness from the inside out."

She snapped her fingers. "I'll tell you one more thing I *can* teach you. I'm finishing up my preparations for the Seder tonight. Would you like to learn what Passover is about? Your aunt Beth is even coming tonight to learn."

I nodded. "Oh yes, I'd love to know."

"Why are you doing a Seder and inviting Christians if you're not Jewish anymore?" Rachel asked.

Davina put her arm around Rachel. "I will always be Jewish. Now when I celebrate Passover I see Yeshua, that is, Jesus, in the Passover, too. It reminds me that Jesus came to be the Messiah for both Jewish people and Gentiles." She saw the look on my face and clarified. "Gentiles are non-Jewish people. There's a lot to learn from the Passover about the way God relates to us," she finished. "This is why Jed invited his mom and dad to come tonight, along with some members of my Messianic fellowship."

"I'd love to learn, then," I said. It was all so interesting! After having been at Sarah's church, and even Grandpa's church, I realized that I understood almost nothing at all about Christianity.

"I'm going to sit over here while you show her," Rachel said in a kind of sullen voice as she wandered into the living area. "I already know everything I need to know about Passover. I'm going home to celebrate it with my parents and with *Bubbie* tonight."

I heard the sting in her voice. *Um, I think I'll just stay out of this one.*

"I'd love to celebrate it with you and with Bubbie again sometime," Davina said. She didn't take offense, just motioned me toward her as Rachel sat on the couch and thumbed through a magazine.

She looked at the clean table. "Passover is one of the most important holidays for Jewish people. First you have to clean your whole house the week before Passover. You get it all tidy, and you especially have to make sure there's nothing made with leaven, like yeast, *chametz,* in your house. Leaven represents sin."

Davina tickled me with her feather duster. "It's not easy to clean it all up. That's why I spent the night at Bubbie's last night, cleaning it all top to bottom for her. She's too old to get in some of those corners. I hauled all the leaven things away for her."

Rachel dropped her magazine.

"You okay?" Davina asked.

Rachel nodded, picked up the magazine, and kept reading.

"Then we read some scriptures—some from the Torah, the first five books of the scriptures, and from the rest of the Jewish Bible. Jewish people believe in the Old Testament. Jewish believers in Yeshua and Gentile Christians take that legacy and believe that God added the New Testament, too."

Oh! So my little New Testament was only *half* of the Bible.

Davina tapped the Bible next to the head of the table.

"What's this?" I picked up a little round cap from the center of the table.

"A *yarmulke,* a skullcap," Davina said. "Jewish men wear them as a sign of respect to God."

I saw some large crackers stacked in the center of the table. Davina saw my gaze.

"Matzo," she said.

Aha! Now I knew what Rachel was talking about

when she wrote in an email that she was flat as a matzo. Clever!

"Our people wrap three pieces of the matzo in a special kind of cloth—a pouch, really, with three compartments. A piece of matzo goes into each compartment. The middle piece is broken and hidden away. At the end of the evening, the children go to find that missing piece, and the child who finds it is given a special prize."

She held out the matzo to me, three pieces. "Why three?" I asked.

"Jewish people don't agree on a specific meaning, actually," she said. "It's just the way we've celebrated this for thousands of years. However, those of us who know that Yeshua is the Messiah see the truth God foreshadowed long ago." She touched the top matzo, "God the Father," then she touched the middle matzo, "God the Son," and finally the third one, "God the Holy Spirit."

She broke the middle matzo. "Do you know what the Bible teaches us about Jesus? That His body was broken for us, to pay for the sins of many. It is hidden away, in the tomb, and when it is found at the end, by those of us willing to have childlike faith in the Messiah, we have a sweet reward. Salvation and a relationship with Him from that moment on."

Rachel peeked over the top of her magazine. I

could see her, but I didn't give her away. She didn't look happy. Or mad. Curious, and maybe sad.

Davina lifted some parsley from the plate. "Our people dip this into salt water to remind us of the tears of our slavery under the Egyptians, which God freed us from. Christians do it to remind us of the slavery of trying to do everything right, yet still being slaves to sin. Doing what we *want* to do instead of what we know is right."

I gasped. Could she know that was exactly what I was doing with this summer camp thing? That statement seemed aimed right toward me.

If it wouldn't have been rude, I would have joined Rachel on the couch with a magazine. Part of me didn't want to find out any more.

Davina pointed out the other things on the plate. "This is some bitter herbs, and here is a sweet mix of apples and honey."

"*Haroseth!*" Rachel called from behind the magazine. She didn't look up.

Davina smiled. "It reminds us that there are sweet times in serving God, too. And that He brings sweetness into our lives along with sorrow."

I couldn't help myself. "Like your wedding? I mean, you're happy to be marrying Jed, but are you sad about, you know. . . ?" I stopped all of a sudden, afraid I'd gone too far.

"I'm having it in a hotel and not a church. I want

my family to be comfortable. But I want them to understand my joy in the Messiah, too.

"Believing in Yeshua doesn't make me not Jewish," she said, talking more toward the magazine hiding Rachel's face than to me. "It just means I am a completed Jew."

She ate a bit of the sweet mix with the bitter one and invited me to do the same. Inside, I was quaking. I was shaking. Something was happening to me that was not related to flowers or apples.

As I ate that mix, and the sweetness of the honey coated my tongue but didn't completely protect it from the sharpness of the bitter herbs, I began to understand something.

I wasn't Jewish, but I wasn't completed, either.

"This is the last thing I'll show you," Davina continued. "I know Jake will be back soon to pick you girls up." She picked up a bone. "Lamb bone. For Passover each family would have to take a lamb into their home and care for it, then after a few days slay it."

I recoiled from the bone. "Kill it?" It seemed kind of barbaric to me.

"When our people were about to be freed from slavery in Egypt," Davina said, "we were commanded to kill a lamb and to smear its blood above and to the sides of the doors." She finished, "Yeshua was the final Passover lamb—He's now no longer a lamb but is our Shepherd instead! Because of Him you can be free, if you want to. You, me, Jed, anyone who asks him. Ruchel even!"

"Ruchel? Rachel?" I was kind of confused.

Davina nodded. "When Jewish children are born, they are often given a Hebrew or Yiddish name besides an English version of it. In our family it's kind of a blessing name. Let's see, Kylie. Hmm. Rachel—how about 'Katriel'?"

Rachel slapped the magazine down. "Sounds good. *Katriel*, we'd better go. Jake will be here soon. I don't want to get in trouble. I don't want anyone to be mad at me."

I heard the doorbell ring.

"Love you." Rachel kissed Davina and hopped outside like the carpet was on fire.

"Love you, too." Davina kissed her back and then kissed my cheek, too.

Rachel made very little small talk on the way home—I think she was preoccupied with her big celebration that night. I think all that talk at Davina's had made her nervous for some reason. I hoped we hadn't bored the sweat out of her. Rachel already knew all of that, obviously. I felt like a bad friend for monopolizing the time. I took advantage of the silence, though, by chatting along the way with Jake.

"I brought you another book." Jake handed it to me. "I thought maybe you'd like to email when you finish the book. Kind of like a two-person book club."

I smiled and nodded. After being at Davina's house, I knew I needed to be colored from the inside out—but that *didn't* mean pink in the face from a compliment from a cute guy, or by confusion over whether or not that would be breaking my mom's "no boyfriends" rule.

Rachel walked me to the door. "So—will we even need those garden books? It kind of seems like all we have is daisies."

"Let's come up with the final flower plan," I said, "and email during the week. Then I'll email Aunt Beth so she can order the flowers for the wedding. Even if we don't use other flowers, I'm kind of having fun paging through the book."

"Me too," Rachel agreed, but her eyes were still distant.

"Rachel?" I turned to her before I went into the house. "Davina never told me. What does *Katriel* mean in Hebrew?"

" 'God is my crown,' " Rachel said.

"What does your Hebrew name mean?"

" 'Little lamb,' " she said softly.

I was kind of surprised at the thought that popped into my mind then. *All little lambs need a shepherd. Even Rachel.* But I didn't say it.

CHAPTER SIX
rachel's story

Skullcap *Scutellaria lateriflora*
A slender plant capped with tiny blue or purple flowers, grows on two- to four-foot stems. Preparations made using this flower were used by herbalists for many years to calm anxiety.

—Northwest Gardener's Guide

Calm anxiety?! *As soon as I saw Zayde's skullcap, his yarmulke, on Davina's table and heard her talk about the Passover, my anxiety started growing stronger and stronger.*

—Rachel Cohen

We picked up Kylie, and of course Jake wanted her to sit in the front with him. Oy vey! It's bad enough that your brother has a crush, but when it's with your new friend and you have to actually watch the sorry drama unfold in front of your eyes—*ick*. "Be back in an hour," I'd told him before we left, and he said, yes, he'd be back soon to get us. Time was tight today. It was the first night of Passover, and my mother was planning a big Seder, of course.

Kylie and I walked up to Davina's door. I hadn't been here for a while, not since she was engaged, that's for sure. A doormat lay in front of the door, and two potted red silk geraniums stood on either side. Just like at Bubbie's house.

I don't know why I had the jitters. Finally I just pushed the doorbell. Within seconds Davina opened the door to us.

"Welcome!" Davina enveloped me in a deep hug and then hugged Kylie, too. Her hair was tied back in a French chignon—the *exact* hairdo that I wanted to try. Looking at it on her, I knew it would look good on me. Hey—what was she wearing?

"I recognize that! That's Aunt Momo's apron!" I said. I guess there was no reason she couldn't wear it, of course. Momo was her mother, after all.

"You're right!" Davina said. "She always wears it to get ready for Passover, and I am, too."

What? Davina was celebrating Passover? I—I just

thought she had left that behind. When I'd asked a couple of years ago why she wasn't at the Seder with the
rest of the family, people had waved me off. I had
thought it was because she had refused to come—if
you're not a Jewish person anymore, what's the point?
But I wasn't so sure I wanted to know the answer right
now, either.

"We've been emailing about the flowers and stuff,"
Kylie said. "I know Jed wants it to be a surprise, but we
thought that with you being the bride and all it would be
good if you let us know some of the things you'd like."

I heard Kylie chatting, but I kept looking around the
room. *Who will come to her Seder? What will they do?*

"How sweet!" Davina laughed. "I have to admit, it's
a little strange to turn over the whole flower thing to
Jed, my being the bride and all. But I trust him, and I
know he must have something unusual planned."

Kylie and I smiled at each other.

"Let's sit down at the table here, if you don't mind,"
Davina said. "I had to move the couch up against the
wall so I could extend the table for all of my Passover
guests tonight. I meant to get this all set up earlier, but
I was out late last night."

For the first time I noticed how much like Rachel—
the first Rachel—Davina looked. I wondered if Bubbie,
or my dad or Uncle Sid, thought of that, too, when they
saw Davina. I wonder if they thought that's what the
"original" Rachel might have looked like, all grown up. I

know they thought of her often. Just look at my name.

Davina went into the kitchen and brought back three glasses of pomegranate punch, an old family recipe. I loved it!

After slurping mine down I spoke up. "Kylie brought a notebook; do you want to tell us some of the things you'd like?"

I saw the Passover glasses set by each place setting—gold rimmed ones, like my mother used. It looked identical to what would be on our table tonight. *Do Uncle Sid and Aunt Momo know she still celebrates Passover?!*

Davina sat down in one of her covered wooden chairs. "Well, I think it'd be nice if there were some daisies involved," she said.

Oh man, face, don't fail me now. I refused to look at Kylie, but I heard her breathing go dead quiet. I looked straight ahead.

"That's about all," she said. "Something pretty to carry to the altar, but not too heavy. I had a friend who took up a twenty-five-pound bouquet and almost passed out before the end of the ceremony."

"Nothing heavy," Kylie promised. Then she pointed at Davina's piano. "Do you play?"

I looked over and saw the photos all lined up, just like at Bubbie's house. I walked over and looked at them. There was my family, and Bubbie and Zayde—in Israel. Zayde had one of his woven skullcaps on, and they stood in front of the Wailing Wall.

My heart pinged, like sonar going out and finding nothing to bounce up against. Did Davina know that Bubbie had taken her picture down?

"I do play some," Davina said. "Most of our family is musical." She reached over and rumpled my hair. "This little woman is quite a clarinetist," she said.

I couldn't stand it. After Dad and I had a big blowout on the way home from Mrs. Rosenthal's house about if I could or could not quit clarinet, I had refused to play. Dad and I had made a silent truce for Passover—he didn't bring it up and neither did I. It hurt to have it between us, and what was worse was there was so much more there. Was I going to bring up the summer job with things this way? No. I wanted no more trouble between me and Dad. But I wasn't backing down, either. I didn't want to talk about clarinet at all. Here, there, or anywhere.

I spied an opportunity to change the subject. "What are those?" I pointed out the flowers in a small glass bubble vase in the center of the partially set table.

Davina laughed. "We made those in class this week. I taught my kindergartners how flowers drink. We took some white daisies"—she smiled—"naturally, and cut their stems down. Then I set some in a glass thick with pink food coloring, some in a glass with yellow, with blue, etc. When we were done, we had a bouquet of beautiful flowers and a science lesson sneaked in to boot!"

"I wish you were one of *my* teachers!" Kylie said.

I looked at her face, full of joy, her "Maid Marian" hairstyle. I saw why Jake liked her. I wanted to get to be better friends with her. She seemed to be able to handle emotional maturity without sending a grenade off in every direction like I did.

Davina snapped her fingers. "I'll tell you one more thing I *can* teach you," she said to Kylie. "I am finishing up my preparations for the Seder tonight. Would you like to learn what Passover is about? Your aunt Beth is even coming tonight to learn."

Kylie nodded. "Oh yes, I'd love to know."

I couldn't stand it. She wouldn't celebrate Passover with us but was having all these Christians over? "Why are you doing a Seder and inviting Christians if you're not Jewish anymore?" I burst out.

Davina put her arm around me, and I felt her love and warmth radiate through her skin and into mine. All the years we spent together as cousins came rushing back to my mind. She always took time to include me, to play dolls. She never let the older kids leave me out. She passed down her very best clothes to me, making sure to keep them in good shape so I would be able to wear the clothes I always envied.

"I will always be Jewish," she said to me in a soothing voice. "Now when I celebrate Passover, I see Yeshua, Jesus, in the Passover, too. It reminds me that Jesus came to be the Messiah for both Jewish people and Gentiles." She looked at Kylie, who looked confused. "Gentiles are non-Jewish people. There's a lot to learn from the Passover about the way God relates to us," she finished. "This is why Jed invited his mom and dad to come tonight, along with some members of my Messianic fellowship."

What is a Messianic fellowship? No. I didn't want to know.

Yes I did. I'd look it up online.

"I'd love to learn, then," Kylie said. Of course she did. She was a Christian. Why wouldn't she?

"I'm going to sit over here while you show her." I headed toward the couch. I wasn't going to sit by and hear my faith and the faith of my people ripped. But I didn't want to be rude to my cousin and my friend, either. "If that's okay. I already know everything I need to know about Passover. I'm going home to celebrate it with my parents and with *Bubbie* tonight."

I meant that to sting.

"I'd love to celebrate it with you and with Bubbie again sometime," Davina said as she looked at the clean table. "Well, first you have to clean your whole house the week before Passover. You get it all tidy, and you especially have to make sure there's nothing made with leaven in your house. In the Bible, leaven represents sin."

She tickled Kylie with her feather duster. "It's not easy to clean it all up. That's why I spent the night at Bubbie's last night, cleaning it all top to bottom for her.

She's too old to get in some of those corners. And I hauled all the leaven things away for her."

I dropped my magazine. Davina hadn't meant that to sting, but it did. She hadn't changed, not really. She still loved Bubbie and was still doing things to honor her and her beliefs, too. My eyes filled with tears. I felt ashamed of the things I had thought about Davina and about my bellyaching about helping Bubbie clean up.

And ... Davina must have noticed that her picture wasn't there.

"You okay?" Davina asked me.

I nodded but didn't look at her, unwilling to let her see my eyes or to let the tears spill. Instead, I picked up the magazine and pretended to keep reading.

She explained about the Torah, and the Bible, and how she now believes that God gave both the Old Testament, which I usually called the Old Covenant, and the New Covenant, which I know Christians call the New Testament. Christians, and I guess some Jewish people. Like her.

"What's this?" Kylie picked up a yarmulke from the center of the table.

"A yarmulke, a skullcap," Davina said. "Jewish men wear them as a sign of respect to God."

It was one of Zayde's skullcaps, here! I'd recognize it anywhere. My dad would wear one tonight. Jake would, too.

I pretended to dive into the magazine article again.

As if I had any idea what it was actually about.

"Matzo," Davina said, holding up a piece of the cracker bread I loved. "Our people wrap three pieces of the matzo in a special kind of cloth—a pouch, really, with three compartments. A piece of matzo goes into each compartment. The middle piece is broken and hidden away. At the end of the evening, the children go to find that piece, and the child who finds it is given a special prize."

She broke the middle matzo. "Do you know what the Bible teaches us about Jesus? That His body was broken for us, to pay for the sins of many. It is hidden away, in the tomb, and when it is found at the end, by those us of willing to have childlike faith in the Messiah, we have a sweet reward. Salvation and a relationship with Him from that moment on."

I couldn't help it. I looked at them over the top of my magazine. Interesting—no one I knew had a solid explanation about why there were three matzos in the *echad*. Why was the middle one broken? Why was the *afikomen,* the broken piece, hidden away and then returned with great joy?

We did the same ritual year after year, holding it as sacred and important. *Why?*

A spidery feeling crept up from my stomach.

"This is some bitter herbs, and here is a sweet mix of apples and honey," Davina said.

"Haroseth!" I shouted from behind the magazine. *If*

you're going to teach her, at least use the right words,
I thought.

Davina smiled; I could hear it in her voice. "It
reminds us that there are sweet times in serving God,
too. And that He brings sweetness into our lives along
with sorrow."

I know that is what Bubbie sometimes thought about
on Passover. The bitterness and sorrow of Zayde's
death, of the death of the first Rachel.

I felt Davina's voice turn toward my direction, and
my face grew hot behind the magazine. "I am a completed Jew. I have completed what the Messiah began
for me. He doesn't want to replace my Jewishness. He
seeks to fulfill it."

A believer in Jesus and still Jewish? I wondered if
Bubbie knew this. If Daddy did. I wondered if they'd
ever heard this Christian stuff about Passover or read
the scriptures in the New Testament that was written by
and for Jewish people, too.

Davina picked up a lamb bone. "For Passover each
family would have to take a lamb into their home and
care for it, then after a few days slay it. Yeshua was the
final Passover lamb—He's now no longer a lamb but is
our Shepherd instead! Because of Him you can be free,
if you want to. You, me, Jed, anyone who asks him.
Ruchel even!"

I snapped back to life when I heard my name in
Yiddish.

"Ruchel? Rachel?" Kylie said. I don't think she'd ever heard my Yiddish, family name.

Davina nodded. "When Jewish children are born, they are often given a Hebrew or Yiddish name besides an English version. Let's see, Kylie. Hmm. Rachel—how about 'Katriel'?"

I'd had just about enough. I couldn't take listening to this anymore. I was worried—more than worried! Not because we were going to be late, but because this could possibly make sense. I slapped my magazine down.

"Sounds good. We'd better go, *Katriel*. Jake will be here soon. I don't want to get in trouble. I don't want anyone to be mad at me."

They chattered on for a few minutes and I hung out by the door, willing myself not to listen, but being so interested that I was already as entangled as I could be.

"Love you." I kissed Davina and raced to the door as soon as the bell rang.

"Love you, too." Davina kissed me back and then kissed Kylie, too.

I hardly talked on the way home. I was stunned into silence. Literally! I had no idea that Davina still thought of herself as Jewish, or that people didn't have to stop being Jewish if they believed in Jesus.

I felt ashamed of digging at her for Bubbie. I felt nervous for even hearing those things.

I had more questions than I knew what to do with—and who would I talk with? No one. *Neyn. Keyner.*

Because I didn't want to know any more than I already knew. If my dad knew what was running around in my head and heart, he'd be more than willing to compromise on the clarinet.

Jake got us home, and we both went to our rooms to change into good, fancy Pesach clothes. My mom had the gold-rimmed Pesach dishes out, and the candles were lit throughout the house. I was so glad that Uncle Sid and Aunt Momo celebrated with her family this year and not ours. Bubbie was here, though.

The Seder began as it always did, with my brother and father putting on their skullcaps—some of Zayde's—and my mother chanting the blessing over the candles that warmed the room with thousands of years of my people's history.

I celebrated and felt real joy. But at each turn I now saw two possible meanings.

Cleaning the chametz out of the house.

Parsley dipped in salty tears.

Haroseth.

The shank bone of the Passover lamb.

CHAPTER SEVEN
kylie's story

Winter Fat *Ceratoides lanata*
A wooly-looking shrub good for forage; long roots make it good for erosion control. Likes chalky soil.
—Northwest Gardener's Guide

Wooly-looking, all right. After a long winter with little exercise, I hoped that my "winter fat" wasn't going to prevent me from getting an ultimate and gorgeous dress for the wedding.
—Kylie Peterson

Shopping date! I glanced at the article I had cut out of the paper and pinned to my bulletin board last month. "Teens Need Independence and Excitement!" And I, for one, was going to have it. I looked at one of the items farther down the list, blushed, and quickly looked away.

Rachel had said to meet her at the front of Nordstrom the next Saturday morning. One week till the wedding! We were going to finish up the last details about the flowers, get anything we needed, and just make sure it was all set. Suddenly I realized how big of a job Jed had really assigned to us. What was he *thinking*? Mom parked the car, and she and Hayley waited with me till Rachel and her mom arrived.

"Hi, so nice to meet you." My mom held her hand out and shook Rachel's mom's hand.

"Likewise!" Rachel's mom was small and dark and pretty. "We're nearly family now," she said. She didn't look rude or mean or like she didn't want us around. My mom looked so tall and thin next to her.

"Put a couple dresses on hold," Mom said to me quietly. "I'm not sure how much we'll have. We can come back in a day or two and pick out the one that works best after I go over the finances."

I nodded. We'd never had tons of money, but my mom sure seemed more concerned with money now than she had been in a long time. Maybe it had to do with those quiet phone calls. Maybe my dad wasn't paying his child support again.

"Jake will pick you up and take you home," Rachel's mom said to Rachel, then turned to my mother. "Would you like my son to bring Kylie home, too? He's got a new car, so he doesn't mind driving all day and all night."

Please, Mom. Say yes. Say YES!

"Sure, if it's not a problem," Mom said.

"It's no problem at all."

"I've got quite a bit to do this afternoon," Mom finished up. "And she assures me that Jake drives safely." Rachel looked intently at her shoe laces. I looked at mine, too, not wanting to catch Jake's mom's eye.

"Can I have a friend over?" Hayley asked in a small voice.

"We'll talk about that later," Mom said in a tired but kind voice.

"Great, great, can we *go* now?" Rachel asked her mother. I nodded my agreement.

"Go, go, Miss Ants-in-the-Pants," her mother said. "Watch the debit card. Don't talk to anyone except a sales clerk. Keep your phone on, and text message me every half hour."

Rachel rolled her eyes but smiled. I smiled, too. I had to keep my phone with me, too. But we were almost fifteen. Okay, we'd be fifteen in half a year.

First stop—coffee. "Let's make a plan," I said.

"Great idea. One of us has to be an adult," Rachel teased. I felt that like an unintentional poke in a bruise, though she couldn't know what it meant to me. I hated being a little adult.

"No, really, I want to have fun, too," I insisted.

We sat down at Seattle's Best Coffee and I whipped out a pad. Over the past week we'd each agreed to come up with one idea for the wedding. I hoped that we hadn't come up with the same one. It might be awkward. I thought I'd let her go first just in case.

"So, what did you come up with?" I chewed the nub of the pen.

"Well, I hope you like it." Her dark eyes sparkled. "Remember how Davina said she wished the kindergarten kids could be involved?"

My heart fell. What if she had *my* idea? "Yes . . ."

"I thought that maybe we could get a picture of each kid in the class and put it in the center of a paper daisy. Then we could stick those on a special board—like poster board or something—and have that in the wedding/reception room. We could buy the paper daisy stuff here, and I could assemble them at home this week before we go. My aunt Momo could go to Davina's class when Davina's gone—she's taking a few days off before the wedding. She could take digital pictures, get them printed, and bring them to us. We'd have to be up late Friday night at the hotel putting them together, but hey—what else is a hotel for? You and me to party!"

"What a fantastic idea!" I said. "You're very creative. I'm afraid my idea isn't quite as original as yours."

"Oh, go on," Rachel said. "What's your idea?" She sipped her mint mocha and made it slurp. Her hair was down again, just straight down her back. If I had hair like that, I'd be doing all kinds of fancy stuff with it.

"Remember those dyed daisies at Davina's?" I sipped my iced latte. "Since she liked them so much—and since the other daisies will be all white—I thought maybe we could dye some of them the night before the wedding and put them in the glass centerpiece bowls with colored glass marbles at the bottom. It would be cheap and colorful and still remind her of her kindergarten kids. If you don't think that's too much, what with your idea and all," I said.

"Not at all. I loved those daisies."

"I couldn't get them out of my mind," I admitted. "We can buy colored glass marbles here today." Aunt Beth had given me some money for supplies. "Then we can put the flowers in plastic buckets from the hotel on Friday night, to dye while we're doing the faces!"

"Great!" Rachel tossed her cup into the garbage and I did likewise. We tooled around the mall for a while and found the colored marbles at a florist shop and the paper for the daisy faces at a craft store.

"You'll call your aunt Beth and tell her about the daisies for the tables and also the flowers we picked out from the gardening books for the bouquet?"

We'd thumbed all the way through the garden books this week and came up with a plan on the phone for the floral bouquets. "Yes," I said. "She'll have to call the supplier today."

We walked down the mall hallway. Was it time to take our friendship to the next level? "I have to pick out a dress. I thought maybe, if you have time, we could do it together?"

Rachel text messaged her mom and brother. "Yeah, he'll be here in about an hour."

I looked at my watch. An hour should be fine. Sarah was coming over tonight.

"What are *you* wearing to the wedding?" I asked as we walked into Macy's.

"I don't know," Rachel answered. "Should we look for me, too?"

I nodded. "Yes! I mean, it's not like we're going to get matchy dresses like little girls, but it would be cool to pick them out together."

"Just a minute." Rachel stepped aside to make a call. I tried not to overhear, but I did just a little.

"Please, Mom, I want to buy a dress with my friend. If you don't like it we can talk later. Please."

There was silence, and then Rachel came back flushed. I didn't ask what the conversation was about, but I could tell by the look on her face that it had worked out okay.

"Let's go!"

We looked through Macy's first, but everything was either too casual or like a prom dress—just a little over the top.

I held up a glittering green strapless number. "What do you think?" I teased.

"I think it's fine if you're Dorothy going to the Emerald City," Rachel joked, and we both burst out laughing.

Rachel held up a dress based on a Harley Davidson biker jacket. "Is it me?"

"Ah, no. Unless there's a Harley Hogs meeting in Victoria next weekend."

She put it back on the rack. "I think my dad would lock me in Rapunzel's tower if I showed up with that." We started walking to Nordstrom. The talk about what kind of dress her dad would and wouldn't like her to wear seemed to be stuck in her thoughts. Finally she blurted out, "My dad is, uh, a little overprotective. About clothes and stuff. Wearing my hair up. Jobs. That kind of thing."

On the way to the store, she told me about her problem. "My dad loves me, and he wants the best for me. But my whole family has been freaked out since my dad's sister died when she was a teenager. I'm named after her. They want to give me the best of everything and protect me. Instead, I feel like I'm swaddled in a cocoon. I want to live my own life. But since my dad won't listen, I end up, um, sneaking around sometimes. I don't know what to do," she confided.

I sympathized with her and listened to her. "I don't know what to tell you," I said. "I do think your hair would look beautiful up, and he does seem a little overprotective. But from my perspective, I wish I had a dad who was willing to watch out for me, even if it was a bit too much."

She smiled at me. "Does your mom have rules?"

"Oh yes," I said. *Like no boyfriends.*

I liked Rachel. She struggled, like I did. I thought we were going to be good, long friends. Cousins, maybe.

In Nordstrom we both struck gold.

"Looooook!" She held up a midnight blue dress. It wasn't really satin, but it was soft and slightly shiny and folded in all the right places. It had a thin belt that was clasped with a rhinestone buckle.

"That's beautiful," I said. "Do you think blue is a good color for you?"

Rachel laughed. "Not for *me*. For *you*!" She brought it over and held it up.

I looked at it in the mirror. It was truly beautiful. "Kind of medieval, in a contemporary kind of way," I whispered. I looked at the price tag and winced.

"Just hold on to it," Rachel said. I did, poking around the racks for something a bit cheaper. I didn't find anything cheaper, but I did find something drop-dead gorgeous in cranberry.

"Look at this!" I held it up. It had thick straps that met in a princess cut top and a thin skirt—not body hugging, but not baggy, either. Very grown up. I held it against Rachel. "Oh, Rachel, the color is great on you," I said. She looked in the mirror and drew in her breath.

"It's perfect. It's . . . perfect," she said.

We ran into the dressing rooms, side by side, and I shimmied into mine. *Please* let it fit. I would do five hundred crunches a day between now and Saturday if I needed to. *Please don't let my upper arms look like flubba.*

I came out of the dressing room and so did Rachel.

"We're it," I said. For the first time, I felt like a beautiful girl.

"Let's put them both on hold," she said, nodding her agreement.

We put them on hold and went to a less expensive department store, too. We each picked another dress. I found a black one with tiny pink flowers scattered across it; very nice—but no oomph. Rachel found a light blue dress that had little darts in the waist. It was beautiful, but kind of young looking. We put them on hold, too.

"Time to meet Jake at Seattle's Best," she announced after looking at her phone. "He's there."

I felt my heart squeeze. *I wonder what he'd think of the midnight blue dress?*

Give it up. It's too much money. I sighed and called my mom on the way to tell her we'd be home soon and to remind her that Sarah was coming over tonight.

On the way to the coffee place, I told Rachel about Sarah. "You'd like her," I said. "She's extremely fun. She set up wacky canoe races at school last year. And she's the one who first started talking to me about God."

Rachel looked at me. "What do you mean?"

My stomach felt like it was full of wriggling worms. My mouth wouldn't open. Rachel had told me the truth about her problems, and I owed it to her to do the same.

"Sarah's family is kind of religious, like my aunt

Beth and Jed," I finally said. "But not in a bad, pushy way. In a kind, 'We want you to be happy and content and excited, too,' way."

"Is your family like that?" Rachel asked.

I shook my head. "Rachel, I'm not even sure I *am* a Christian."

"What does it mean to be a Christian? I'm confused."

"I think I was, too. In fact, after listening to what Davina said last week, I'm pretty sure I'm not. I don't trust Jesus like that. I don't know Him like that, either. I'd thought being a Christian was like being American, you know? Born that way. But now I know that's not true, and I'm kind of panicked about it."

Rachel slowed way down. "Oh. That's heavy. I never understood that."

"Me neither." I explained about summer camp and the job and how Hayley could go. "I guess I'm not sure what they meant," I said. "Or maybe I know but don't want to admit it."

Rachel patted my arm. "Maybe you should talk with your friend Sarah about it?"

I nodded but didn't really agree. Sarah's family was so perfect. Sarah thought I was a Christian. Maybe she'd think I had been lying to her all along. Maybe she'd think I wasn't good anymore. "Maybe."

Rachel nodded as we arrived at Seattle's Best

Coffee. Jake sat at a table looking really cute. His hat was on backward, and he'd let his hair grow a little long over the ears, like most of the guys at my school. He had guy flip-flops on and jeans and a blue shirt that showed off his eyes. I smiled and tried *very hard,* but unsuccessfully, to remember that a *first love* had also been listed in the newspaper article.

"Oh!" Rachel said as we arrived. "I forgot something. Do you guys mind if I run and get it while you hang out here for a few minutes?"

"Sure," I said. I didn't dare look at her, I'd smile for sure. *I owe you one.*

"Can I buy a coffee for you?" Jake asked.

"Sure," I answered. My face grew hot. The worms wriggled. Was this official dating behavior? If so, it was definitely off limits to me. No misunderstanding about that.

Maybe it was just friendliness.

My heart beat fast. *Ka-chunk, ka-chunk.* It didn't usually do that when I was with my friendly friends.

Jake came back with a coffee. My second today. I hoped my hands wouldn't shake.

"So what did you think of the book?"

I relaxed. "I really liked it—I felt like I was there," I said. "Did you see some of the historical errors? Like saying that they couldn't wear royal purple?" Okay, I hoped I wasn't sounding like a library nerd.

His face lit up. "Very cool that you saw that. I did, too."

We talked about the book for a while, then the wedding. "I hear they're going to have a band," he said. "Davina loves music."

"She told me that your family is very musical."

"Are you?"

I shook my head. "No. But I'd like to learn how to hip-hop dance," I admitted. *Okay, if he makes fun of me, the whole deal is off. Whatever the "deal" is.*

Instead, he smiled. "Maybe I'll show you next weekend, at the wedding." He turned his cap to the side. "DJ Jazzy Jake."

I laughed and Rachel came back. "All right, you two, we'd better get going."

I looked at my watch. Yeah, definitely. Sarah was going to be at my house in half an hour.

Fifteen minutes later Jake and Rachel dropped me off; when I walked into the house, I had one of Jake's books in my hand. My mom glanced at it and looked at me. I turned away.

"Wow—the house looks great!" I said too brightly. The blinds were all drawn up; the spring light slid through the panes and lit up the room. Each and every corner of the house sparkled, and there were bunches of spring flowers in vases sprouting in almost every room. "I didn't even know we owned vases."

"Ha-ha," Mom said. "You're not the only one with a floral knack these days. I wanted the house to feel homey when Sarah comes over. A couple of packs came in from Netflix with some movies for you guys to choose from. I also bought stuff to make homemade caramel corn."

"Wow, Mom. You've turned into Martha Stewart." I love homemade caramel corn. It tastes nothing like Cracker Jacks.

"Hardly," she said dryly. "But I'm trying. Tell me about your shopping trip." She patted the seat next to her.

"Oh, Mom, I found the most wonderful dress! It's midnight blue and it shimmers—but not too much. It's grown-up but not low cut. You'll love it."

"I can't wait to see it. . . . And how much was it?"

I told her and she didn't flinch. Maybe there was hope! I told her about the second-choice black dress, too.

"Well, we'll talk about it later, maybe pick one of them up tomorrow. I have a couple of free hours in the morning."

"How did work go today?" I asked, trying not to pry but not wanting curiosity to kill me, even though I am allergic to cats. What were all those closeted phone calls about? Had Hayley really heard something strange a couple of weeks ago?

"Not well," she said. "I think we're losing that client."

I waited for it. "If we do, *I'm dead.*" It never came. Nothing.

Hayley walked in the room. "Ready to play checkers?" she asked my mom.

Just then the doorbell rang and I ran to open the door.

"Hey!" Sarah had on some new embroidered jeans, a gathered peasant shirt, a wrist full of bangles, and boots. Only she could get away with that combo. It looked fantastic.

"Hey yourself," I said. "Come on in."

Sarah closed the door behind her, and we ran down to my room and closed that door, too. "Did you find a dress?"

"Totally." I told her about our shopping trip and trying on dresses. Sarah looked kind of sad.

"And then Jake and I had coffee," I continued. We sat down on my bed, and I told her about the Maid Marian book and our discussion and what Jake was wearing. I even mentioned the *ka-chunk, ka-chunk.* My dog, Missy, had followed us into the room. I patted her on the head. "Do you like Jake?" I asked the dog. "Do you think he's to die for?"

I grabbed a dog treat from the dish on my dresser and waved it up and down in front of her.

Missy nodded her agreement. "Do you think I should talk to Mom about Jake?" I waved the biscuit back and forth, and Missy shook her head, "No." Then she gobbled the treat.

Sarah giggled. "Nice try." She sat there for a minute, kind of staring into space.

"Are you okay?" I asked.

"Oh yeah," she said. "It's just kind of weird that you have a boyfriend. I thought it wouldn't happen to us till we were older, and that it would happen to us together."

I sucked in my breath. "Do you think that Jake is a boyfriend already?"

"What do you think?"

"I guess so. I'm not really allowed to have a boyfriend yet, though."

"Me neither. So what are you going to do?"

I had to *do* something? "I don't know." I shrugged. Truth is, I didn't want to do anything. Liking Jake and having him like me made me feel great.

Sarah looked like she was about to tell me something, but then she must have changed her mind.

We talked about the dresses and what jewelry I could wear, and we painted our nails. Sarah swirled white on top of my colored nails and pricked it with a pin so it looked like flowers.

"You are so good," I said and painted hers back,

though not as nicely. I just wasn't too artistic, even though she'd shown me how to do it once.

After the movie was over we walked down the hall toward the kitchen to make the caramel corn. On the way I could see Hayley and Mom giggling on Mom's bed. The phone rang, and Mom answered it and went into her bathroom to talk, closing the door behind her.

"How's your sister?" Sarah asked.

"Oh, she's got the plague," I said. "Not really. She just thought that last week. She's okay. She really liked your church."

"Then she'll love camp! Would you guys like to come to church tomorrow?" Sarah asked. "I like it so much better when you're there. I feel like we haven't seen a lot of each other lately, with this wedding and all. We used to go biking and have coffee and text message and stuff."

I nodded. "I miss you, too. But we're supposed to pick up my dress tomorrow morning."

Plus, I just wasn't ready to talk with Ben, the camp director. What I really wanted to say was, "Hey, what *is* a Christian to you guys? What kind of strange talk was in that letter?" But I was embarrassed.

Sarah didn't push me. "I guess that's okay. I'm here tonight, right? And we'll be seeing a lot of each other over the summer."

We walked into the kitchen and started the popcorn in the microwave. I stirred the sugar and corn
syrup and butter in a pan till it was boiling, and
Sarah took the popcorn out of the microwave,
poured it into a bowl, and salted it with dry roasted
peanuts. We poured the syrup over the mix,
spooned it out on cookie sheets, and stuck it into
the oven to bake.

"What's this?" Sarah pointed to the glass marbles. I'd left all my shopping gear on the kitchen
counter.

"Oh! So cool! Let me show you. It's for the
wedding."

I ran down the hall. Mom was still on the phone
in the bathroom, and Hayley was thumbing through
the cartoons on TV while she waited. Hayley was
wearing her little daisy-chain wreath, even though
it had dried out.

I guess I couldn't ask my mom if I could use one
of her bouquets or not. I'd just use one of the glass
vases and the flowers she'd set out. She wouldn't
mind. I headed back to the kitchen.

"First you put some of these glass marbles into
the bottom of the vase." I tipped the mesh bag, and
some marble chunks tumbled noisily into the vase,
like ice cubes clinking together.

"Then you pour in some water and some food
coloring." I filled the vase with water, then dripped

in orange food coloring and stuck in some white flowers

"We'll come back and see what happens right before we take you home."

Sarah and I went back to my room and chatted about school and our friends and our plans for the summer. "Um, Kylie? You know how we were talking about Jake? Well, there's a guy at church that I really like. I mean, I like him more than the others."

Oh. I felt kind of sad that we hadn't spent enough time together for me to already know this. "Next time I go, I'll check him out and give you the thumbs-up or down," I said.

"He'll be at the camp training meeting," she said. "And he'll be with us this summer, too. I'll be watching how you handle the Jake situation for some tips. Christians are supposed to learn from one another," she teased, but I caught a note of truth in her voice.

It hit me, right then, for sure.

I am not a Christian. I wasn't.

I knew it, but Sarah didn't. I was so embarrassed, because I'd thought all along that I was one, and now I knew I really wasn't. Had the teacher couple at Sarah's church said something about that? I'd slipped the bulletin into my little Bible that week. When Sarah left I would look it up.

I wished at that moment that I was a strong

enough person to just tell her, but I wasn't. I wanted her to like me; I wanted her to think I was as good as she was. I wanted us to be equals.

"Hey!" Sarah interrupted my thoughts. "What's burning?"

We raced into the kitchen and pulled the caramel corn from the oven. "It's a bit, um, overdone," I giggled.

"We'll pick through it," she said. We tossed it into a bowl and ran back to my room to chat and call some other friends on the phone. We had a popcorn fight with the burnt bits and a few stuck in our hair, but we laughed anyway.

"Quick, clean it up before my mom comes in. She cleaned today!" We scurried to find the kernels on the floor, and those we couldn't get to Missy helped out with, tongue flicking, tail wagging.

At a little before ten Mom knocked on the door. "Time to take Sarah home."

"Sure you don't want me to pick you up tomorrow morning?" she asked.

"Thanks anyway," I said. "Hey! I want to show you the flower thingy!" I was eager to teach *her* something for a change!

When we got to the kitchen the flower petals were inky orange, marker-dark at the tips and blushing lighter as they each kissed the center.

"How pretty!" Sarah said.

"Yeah, they're changing from the inside out," I said. "When I was at Davina's the other day, she was telling us that's how it is for *real* Christians. God lives inside you and changes you from the inside. It's not just changing how you act or what you say or whatever. You spend time drinking Him in and then He changes you, and you really become an orange flower, not just one with orange painted on." I stopped for a minute and grinned. "I added that last part myself."

Sarah stood there, looking at me. "Kylie, that is one of the coolest things I have ever heard. I think you're a natural teacher. Can I keep one of these flowers?"

"Yep," I said, feeling smug.

We drove Sarah home, and then I snuggled on the couch with my mom for a few minutes before bed.

"Are you sad that I'll miss some of Mother's Day next weekend when I'm at the wedding?" I asked.

Mom shook her head. "No. I'm taking the weekend off to spend time with Hayley, so you'll be free to enjoy yourself!"

Suddenly I felt jealous of my mom's time with Hayley. "I've been so busy getting ready for the wedding, I feel like I never get any of your time," I said. "I miss you."

"I miss you, too, Kyls," Mom said. "We'll have some time together the next week. Hayley can play with a friend, and you can tell me all about the wedding and give me a nice neck rub."

I smiled. My mom used to pay me a dollar for fifteen minutes of a neck rub when she was stressed from work. "Deal. But I charge more now."

"Oh, you do, do you? Now that you have your big summer job?" We walked into the kitchen together to shut off the lights. "Would you like to keep these flowers in your room?" She held up the little glass vase with the orange swizzle stick bouquet.

I nodded. Mom kissed me good-night, and then I went into my room and she went to tuck in Hayley.

Once in my room, I sat on my bed. I sighed. Then I dug out that little Bible. Oh no, the lesson sheet wasn't in there anymore! I remembered it had been big. I'd pitched it on the way out of church.

Sarah's church. She was always so kind to bring me, and if I was going to be totally honest, I had to admit that the reason I hadn't said anything to her wasn't because she was perfect. It was because I wanted to pretend to be. And I didn't want to deal with the consequences that I knew facing the truth would bring. In my mind, in my heart, I opened the closet door and let everything out.

I sat on my bed some more, Bible in hand, sighing again, staring at the orange flowers and feeling bittersweet. It was cool to be able to share that with

Sarah, but I felt kind of like a poser. I wished I had told her the whole truth.

In fact, I wished I hadn't told her that lesson. *Bragger,* I berated myself. *Faker.*

I opened the Bible up and read the bullets on the inside cover.

- "But now God has shown us a different way of being right in his sight—not by obeying the law but by the way promised in the Scriptures long ago. We are made right in God's sight when we trust in Jesus Christ to take away our sins." Romans 3:21–22

I was so tired of always trying to be perfect and follow every law and rule and plan that I thought made me look like a good person and would make everyone like me.

I read the next bullet:

- "My sheep recognize my voice; I know them, and they follow me." John 10:27

"I'm just a girl, Lord. I'm tired of leading, because I don't even know the way even when I pretend to. My name isn't Rachel, it's Kylie, but I'm still a little lamb. Please live inside me, be my Shepherd. I am willing to be your sheep."

I sank into my bed, and the pillow curved around and hugged me. I felt warmth pipe through me. Peace and joy washed through me. I lay there for a long time, floating in the feeling of contentment. I knew who I would share this with first, all the details, not missing any. Sarah.

But then I sat up. Fear washed through me, too. I had decided to become someone new tonight. I was no longer in charge, and because of that I knew there were going to be changes. Even telling Sarah the good news would bring about change.

Changes were never easy.

I hoped that they wouldn't come real soon.

CHAPTER EIGHT
rachel's story

Mayday Tree *Prunus padus commutata*
Medium-height tree with bright green foliage that
begins to appear in April but continues through the
season through deep green, yellow, and blood red.
Related to the chokecherry.
                                —Northwest Gardener's Guide

There are times in your life when you want to
call "Mayday." Help! Help! You hope someone will rescue
you, but you realize there is absolutely no way out—
you're going down. Yeah, related to chokecherry. Choking
is a good way to describe it.
                                —Rachel Cohen

The waiting car's exhaust sent steam into the still-dark morning. "So we've had a week to get all the details done, and now when we're ready to pull out of the driveway you remember something in the house?" My mom flapped around as she usually did when we were getting ready to leave. I saw Jake trying to hold back a smile. My dad rubbed his temples. He'd had to pack not only for the wedding but for the convention he was leaving for early Sunday morning.

"Ma, I'm sorry. It's important, okay? It's the paper daisies." I hopped out of the car and ran into my room, took the folder from my desk, and ran back into the garage. The *Clipper* to Victoria left at eight in the morning. We had to be there by seven to check in, show our passports, and board. I'd tried, you know? I'm just not a detail girl.

We pulled out of the garage and down the street, then onto the highway toward Seattle. In twenty minutes we curbed at the docks.

I scanned the line for Kylie. "There she is!" I elbowed Jake. "With her aunt Beth and uncle Andy." Jed and his best man had gone the day before, and Davina and her bridesmaid had been in Victoria for two days. Jed's sister went to school in Canada, so she was driving over. Uncle Sid and Aunt Momo had gone up with Davina. The *Clipper* is a passenger-only ferry, so everyone walks on. It's kind of like a floating airplane. I mean, there are both rows of seats and places with tables inside. The tables were the best. You could buy snacks on board, though I didn't think I'd want anything this early, and we'd be in Victoria in a couple of hours.

Looking over the crowd, I wondered if any of these people were Jed and Davina's friends. Of course, friends could always come over tomorrow, too. There would be about fifty guests total. I sighed. Only one important person was missing: Bubbie.

Kylie waved. She looked at me, then Jake. *Oh boy*.

"I'll save you a seat," Kylie mouthed to me.

I nodded and helped my mom with her bags. "Why we have to travel halfway around the world for a wedding, I'd like to know," my mother grumbled.

"*Mother,* it's only a couple of hours. And we're doing it because Davina always dreamed of getting married in Victoria. When someone canceled, she got a break."

"It's about time she got a break of some sort," my mother admitted. "At least the weather is nice. And so is she," she finished graciously.

The boat bobbed in the water as we boarded. Kylie held down a table for us right behind her aunt and uncle. "Come on!" I headed in that direction.

"I'm Andy Apprich." Kylie's uncle held out his hand toward my dad.

"Isaac Cohen."

"Please, sit with us." Uncle Andy moved over.

I thought about Uncle Andy and Davina's Passover. I snuck a look at my dad. He was smiling. *Oy*.

We took the other table, and Kylie broke out a deck of cards as we reveled in the fact that all three of us got to miss school today. Some little kids in the front played at the kiddie toy area at the bow of the boat. An old lady in the row next to us ordered duty-free perfume. *Phew.* I didn't think she needed any more.

We three played cards while we crossed the water. Two hours later we steamed into Victoria. We hopped two cabs to the Empress hotel, rising in the distance, the royalty of resorts. Kylie rode with us, while Jake went with Aunt Beth and Uncle Andy to help with their gear. As the parents of the groom, they had more stuff to carry. I thought Kylie looked a little disappointed when they split up. Watching Jake and Kylie was definitely interesting. Did my mother know? Did *Kylie's* mother know?

"There it is," Kylie whispered to me. "Did you know that the Queen of England stays there when she visits?"

"Do you think they'll give us her room?" I teased.

"Sure, why not?"

Both of us grew quiet. The hotel was a stone castle enthroned in the middle of town. The wind and rain of the century had aged the face a bit. Tiny vines ran up and down the whole four stories of it, kind of like tiny age lines on an older lady. Because it was May, the vines were beginning to uncurl budding ivy leaves. So pretty!

Our cab pulled up right outside of the hotel, and a valet opened the door for us while my dad paid. Tulips were sprinkled across the grass like confetti. Jake was waiting on the curb, along with Aunt Beth and Uncle Andy.

"Coming with us, my dear?" Aunt Beth asked Kylie.

She nodded. "Call me in half an hour and we'll make a plan."

Just like Kylie—making sure there was a plan. Davina didn't know how lucky she was that Kylie was along for this flower surprise. I might have the artistic touch—I'd planned the flowers for the bouquet, mostly—but Kylie would make sure it all got done.

We checked in and took the elevator upstairs to our suite—*suite!* All of our rooms had been upgraded because we were a part of a wedding package.

Oh man. I wanna get married here, too.

Regular Joes like us stayed here. Rich people stayed here. Rich people like those who went to the yacht club during the summer. Suddenly I wondered if I'd applied enough deodorant this morning. I was very sweaty. I hadn't thought about the summer job situation in like, oh, fifteen minutes.

We finally opened the door to our suite. On the right-hand side was a double bedroom, a whole hotel room. It was done up in forest green with deep oak wood and had tiny little topaz bottles of high-class shampoos shimmering on a pond-like mirror on the marble bathroom counter.

"I get the bed by the TV." Jake threw his stuff on that bed.

"Fine," I said. "I get to pick the shows after ten."

"You don't get to pick *any* shows. I'm older."

I threw my stuff on the bed and tossed a pillow in his general direction. "Take the plastic bag off your head. You obviously need more oxygen, as your brain isn't functioning well."

He put his hat on. "I'm going to see if Jed wants any help."

"Jed hardly knows you. You're just trying to get over by their suites. And Kylie."

He laughed at me. "Jed and I go waaaay back." But he didn't deny why he was going over there.

I scooted into my mom and dad's room—well, a suite of its own, really. It was right next to our room, connected by a short, private hallway. Their room had a small living room with a pull-out bed and then a separate bedroom, too. On the table of the living room were two little chocolate turtles swimming across a china plate—and someone had even made faces on them. I beheaded one. Mmmm.

"Just help yourself," Mom teased.

My phone rang. "Hey, it's me," Kylie said. "Aunt Beth is going to do some stuff for a few hours and then she's going to meet with us about the flowers. Since we can't do anything with them till tomorrow morning, do you want to tool around downtown? Maybe get a Mother's Day gift for our moms?"

Mother's Day! I had almost forgotten. It was this Sunday, and Daddy wouldn't even be here. "Lemme check." I turned to my parents. "Can Kylie and I go downtown?"

My dad opened his mouth to say no, but I caught Mom's eye and she answered, "For a few hours. Then you'll have to stick around the hotel to help, and the rehearsal dinner is tonight. Keep your phone on. Don't go more than three blocks." She looked at my dad. "We're in Canada, after all, dear. It's safe."

Dad closed his mouth, but he looked like he'd just been signed up for dental work.

I met Kylie in the lobby and held up three fingers.

"What is that?" she asked.

"The boy scout pledge. Time for us to go boy scouting."

She giggled. "I've already scouted all I need to." Then Kylie's smiled faded. *Uh-oh.* Trouble in paradise? Well, I could understand. Jake wasn't *my* idea of Mr. Right.

We walked downtown, breathing in the blossom-perfumed air, and chattered about our week.

"You know I got it, don't you?" Kylie said.

I nodded. She was so excited about her dress. We both were.

"I have a little money for accessories, too, because my grandpa gives me ten dollars for every A I earn on my report card," Kylie explained.

Accessories! "I totally forgot."

"I'll help you," she reassured and then looked at the visitor's map of Victoria. "Let's walk to that antique store a couple blocks away and see what we can find."

We got in and browsed, and she picked out some beautiful ruby teardrop earrings for me. They glinted in the sunlight like real jewels.

I frowned. "Will anyone be able to see them? I mean, my hair will cover them up."

"Tuck it behind your ears," she said, doing it for me. "And don't worry if your hair is down. Only brides and queens got to wear their hair down in medieval times. It was a great honor."

Yeah. But I'm not a queen *or* the bride. *Harrumph*.

She found a set of sparkling crystal stars for her own hair. "I'm going to wear it in a braided crown," she said. "If I can reach up and do it."

"I can do it," I offered. "If you want me to."

She smiled. "I'd love it. I wish I could reciprocate." We left the store and bought a box of Victoria Creams for each of our mothers at the famous Rogers' Chocolates. Of course, we had to buy some for ourselves. "Let's eat something different for lunch," Kylie said as she dug her teeth into the soft strawberry cream center of her candy.

"Okay, Miss Daring," I said. We settled on an oyster

bar, and I choked down three oysters before ordering a grilled cheese.

When it came time to pay, Kylie held out some Canadian money. "Know what these are?"

"Let me take a wild guess. Coins. Your grandpa gives you coins for earning a B, right?"

"No, I get nothing for earning a B." She looked sad but smiled anyway. It was good to see her happy. In the month or more since I'd known her, she hadn't seemed this free.

"This one"—she held out a silver coin with a bronze center—"is a toonie." I looked at it. It had a bear in the middle, and it said, "Canada—2 Dollars."

"That one's for me," she said. Then she held out a second coin. "This one is for you."

"Why, 'cause it's only one dollar?"

"Look at the back," she said.

"There's some kind of duck on it," I said.

"It's a loon. The coin is effectively known as a loonie." She grinned, and I threw a roll at her but tucked the coin into my pocket as a friendship treasure.

Next we stopped at Lush. They sold all kinds of scented bath balls that fizz in the tub. We found a floral one that reminded us of daisies and decided to wrap it up and give it to Davina at the dinner tonight.

"Is the dinner going to be fancy?" I knew that the groom's family paid for the rehearsal dinner.

"Nope, fish and chips," she answered. "I was kind of hoping for Indian food."

Say, this was a new side of my normally responsible friend. She shoveled weird food like a bulldozer.

When we got back to my room, we decided we should make the kindergarten faces first, and then tonight after the dinner we'd put the white flowers in colored water. Aunt Beth was picking them up later in the afternoon and keeping them in one of the hotel's coolers.

I had already put together the paper daisies; we just needed to glue in the faces and put them on a board. "Look how cute," I said. "Some look like I used to—with pigtails. My dad still keeps a picture of me with pigtails."

Kylie smiled. "They are all cute." She sighed. "I do get tired of kids, though, sometimes. What with taking care of Hayley all the time and everything."

"You'll have more of that at camp this summer, won't you?" I asked.

Kylie set down her scissors and tape. "I have to tell you something."

"What?"

She looked around. "The other night I prayed and told God that I knew I wasn't a Christian. That I wanted to be one, which I now understood that I needed to choose. And I did it. I talked with God and chose Jesus."

I held my breath. "And?"

"And it was wonderful," she said. "It was right. I'm a

Christian now. But now I have lots of things I don't know what to do about. Like camp. Like Jake," she said in a low tone so my mom wouldn't hear.

"Hey—did someone call my name?" Jake walked into my parents' living room.

Kylie looked at me and mouthed, "Help!"

"Kylie was just wondering if you wanted to go to the pool with us after dinner," I said quickly. She looked at me and smiled.

"Sure," he said.

We walked down to check out the flowers in the cooler. Buckets and buckets of daisies.

"My hands hurt already," Kylie said. "I think I need a massage."

I laughed. "We just might when we're done."

Kylie and I sat in Kipling's restaurant in the hotel. I tried not to get dizzy by avoiding looking at the black and white tiles on the floor. Kylie wrote a list.

"Flowers here. Check. Bouquet flowers here. Check. Daisies for vases on table here, and marbles and food coloring. Check."

She looked up at me. "We have to make those tonight, after fish and chips."

"Check," I teased her back.

"Dresses here, accessorized, Mother's Day gifts purchased."

"Check!" we both said at the same time.

"We're ready," I said. She snapped her list shut.

"Kylie, can I ask you a personal question?"

She nodded hesitantly.

"Are you always this organized? Is it fun for you?"

She let out a long sigh and sipped her Mountain Dew. "I am organized, it's true. But I've been in charge of helping my mom ever since my dad left. So I don't really have a choice."

"What *do* you do for fun?"

"Hang out with Sarah and other friends."

"Do you get to do that very often?" I sipped my Cherry Coke. When I was a little girl I called it Cheery Coke because it made me happy to see all the maraschino cherries inside the cup.

"I'd like to do it more," she said. "But it doesn't look like that will happen."

"What do you dream about?" I asked her. "What do you really *want*?"

"To take hip-hop lessons," she said. "Work at camp this summer. Drive a motorcycle."

I almost choked on my drink. "Drive a *motorcycle*?"

"Not very Maid Marian, is it?" she teased. "But it's true. My mom has a license to drive one, but she hasn't since my dad divorced her." She sipped her Dew. "Maybe I'll settle for a Vespa."

I giggled at the thought of her with a helmet and Ray-Bans but admired her courage to take things head on.

"What do *you* dream of?" she asked.

As if on cue, my phone rang. It was my parents.

"Freedom," I told her, rolling my eyes before I answered.

Late that night, after the rehearsal dinner and after we'd swum in the pool and after we'd lined up lots of buckets with white flowers and food coloring around Kylie's room, we said good-night and went back to our rooms.

Jake flipped channels and my parents chatted in the room next door. I opened the drawer next to my bed table to get out some paper and a pen. There was a Bible in the drawer, too. I slipped it out of the drawer quietly, though Jake was wrapped up in *World Wrestling Entertainment* or something, so I needn't have worried.

I opened the book up to the New Testament, hesitantly. I read a few of the words in the section called John. Then I read some more. It sounded like it had been written by Jewish people, just like Davina said. The people were constantly talking in questions, like everyone I knew and loved did.

I read a second section. *"We have found the Messiah."*

I gasped and flipped forward several pages. Romans. *That* obviously wasn't for Jewish people. It was for Italians. I scanned it.

"I am not ashamed of the gospel, because it is the power of God for the salvation of everyone who believes: first for the Jew, then for the Gentile."

I stopped reading and looked at Jake. He wasn't

looking at me at all. My breathing picked up and I kept reading.

"For in the gospel a righteousness from God is revealed, a righteousness that is by faith from first to last, just as it is written: 'The righteous will live by faith.'"

I recognized those last words. In fact, I'd heard them at temple. The idea of righteous people was very Jewish. I pushed the book back into the drawer, far, far back.

Maybe this *was* for Jewish people. I loved my dad and my mom and my Bubbie very, very much. More than anything.

But so did Davina.

I finally drifted off to sleep but had very troubled dreams all night long.

Saturday morning we woke up and had room service. "Since I'll be gone early tomorrow morning, I thought we'd celebrate Mother's Day today," Daddy said. "I also have a special gift for you and Mom," he said to me. "Something to do later this afternoon. About two hours before the wedding."

"I'm supposed to do something two hours before

the wedding? What if Momo needs me?" My mother swatted his arm, but I could see how pleased she was. I was, too. I loved mother-daughter events.

We dined on macadamia nut pancakes with pineapple syrup and turkey sausage and orange juice and real strong coffee. Then we brought it all out to the hall and called for someone to take the dirty dishes away.

"This is the life," Jake said. "I'm going to live like this when I'm rich."

"Better start saving." My dad whacked Jake's shoulder. "I have some business to attend to, and then we'll go down and see if Sid needs any help."

I quickly threw some sweats on and ran down the carpeted hall to the elevator. Once I got downstairs, I spied Kylie waiting for me. *Oy.* Of course she'd be on time.

"Sorry I'm late," I said.

"You're not late," she answered. "But let's go!"

We sat outside of the cooler and slit stems and wove daisy chains over and over. The morning rolled into afternoon.

"Last week when we were shopping, you asked me what it means to be a Christian," Kylie said. "And I'm just learning more and more. What does it mean to be Jewish?"

I wove the flowers carefully, breathing in the acidic pinchy smell of the daisies. "Well, it's kind of your family. It means you have a history thousands of years old, and you're connected with all of those people. It means you were the first people to know and worship God." I set down one chain and began another.

"You kind of have this, like, brotherhood with any other Jewish person. You understand what they've been through."

"Do you go to church?" Kylie asked.

"We call it temple," I answered. "And we go. Sometimes. Some Jewish people go more than others. Some worship and some just go like it's a club."

"Like church," Kylie said. "But Davina still has all that, right?"

I didn't answer. I didn't know.

We wove and wove, and I was wondering if I could send Jed a bill for this. Good grief! My hands! After another hour Kylie's phone went off. She pulled it out of her purse. "Probably Aunt Beth."

She looked at it. It was a message on her voice mail. "Sarah's number," she said. She listened to the message, went kind of white, and then hung up.

I didn't want to pry. I mean, it wasn't my friend. But she kind of lost her weaving rhythm after that.

"You okay?" I asked. "Your face looks like an underdone marshmallow."

"Puffy?" She rustled up a smile.

"White!" I answered.

"Oh, Sarah left me a message. She wanted me to know that she mentioned the flower illustration to Ben, and he said he thought it was so good that when we

160

got together next Sunday for the kickoff, I could use that as part of my time where I'm supposed to tell people about my Christian life."

"Hmm. What are you going to do?"

"I don't know. I could always say no. But maybe I'm not supposed to. Maybe they'll see that I have something good to share and let me teach this summer."

"Maybe. I mean, that would seem the nice thing to do."

"I know I can't get up there and lie. I know I need to come clean with them, because I feel icky even though a misunderstanding got me into it. I hope I feel strong then."

"Hey," I said. "How about I come, too, and cheer you on?" I mean, it was *one* visit, right?

"I'd love that!" Kylie said. "Okay, if you promise to come, I'll do it. After all, you were there when I heard it the first time. Maybe it's a good thing that I shared that lesson with Sarah after all!" She grinned again.

I nodded uneasily, wondering at what I had just said. *Be bold!* I told myself. But now Kylie was text messaging Sarah that she'd do it and that she was bringing a friend along, too.

While she texted I thought about what she said. *I know I need to come clean with them, because I feel icky even though a misunderstanding got me into it.*

I understood.

We finished the chains and laid them gently on the

cooler floor, to the side, where they wouldn't be stepped on. An hour before the ceremony we'd come back down and arrange them on the chuppah. Jed had promised that he'd keep Davina out of the room.

We raced back upstairs to my mom's room and got the kindergarten photos. Kylie looked around for Jake, and then her face dropped when he wasn't there. Me? I could smell a disaster coming in that direction. Mom held out a chocolate turtle for each of us and said, "There's another surprise in *your* room," to me.

Kylie and I walked into my room. "Bubbie!" I threw my arms around her. "You came!"

"Of course," she said. "Would I miss my own granddaughter's wedding? Nu, that is not going to happen while my legs still work. Of course, they feel like two knishes stuffed into *these*!" She pointed at her pantyhose and snapped them. "But I'll live."

"How did you get here?" I asked.

"I swam," Bubbie teased. "Which is why my hair is a mess. I took the *Clipper* this morning, noodle, and Yitzhak picked me up at the terminal."

I saw Kylie look at me. "Yitzhak is my dad," I explained. "Bubbie, this is my friend Kylie."

Bubbie walked over and kissed Kylie's cheeks. "Any friend of Ruchel must be a wonderful girl."

"She's Jed's cousin, too," I finished and watched her reaction.

Bubbie hesitated just a little and said, "Family is even better, nu?"

Jake had apparently moved his things to the pull-out couch in my parents' parlor so Bubbie could have his bed.

I hoped there wasn't a Christian Bible in the table next to Bubbie's bed, too.

"And now—a nap," Bubbie said. "Apparently Yitzhak has some surprise for me this afternoon. At my age a surprise is not always a welcome thing."

I giggled. "It's a Mother's Day present, Bubbie, and Mom and I are coming, too."

"Then you can pick me up off the floor if the shock is too much," she kidded, then pottered over toward the bed. "Good night for now, Ruchel and Kylie."

"Kylie and I are going to bring the flowers downstairs now," I told my mom. "And put them in the vases and hang up the kindergarten pictures."

My mother nodded and blew me a kiss and then got back on the hotel phone with Aunt Momo.

We walked to Kylie's suite, which was very much like ours. Kylie introduced me to Leeann, Jed's sister, who was sharing a room with her.

She hugged me. "We'll be cousins now," she said as she bustled off to help Davina with some final details.

Kylie and I gathered the flowers into a big hotel laundry bag and ran downstairs to put them into the glass bowls with water before they withered.

It was the first time we'd seen the ballroom. Kylie inhaled. "I see why Davina wanted to get married here," she said.

I nodded. "Me too. Ever since she came to Victoria with her mom and dad one spring break when she was ten she's wanted to be married here. It's kind of cool, especially since that first, um, 'wedding' went so bad, that she got to get her dream come true."

We stood together, bag in hand, and looked around the room. Maroon curtains were held back by golden swags, like barrettes clipping back great expanses of hair. In fact, the entire room had a golden glow to it. The tables were all set up for dinner, and there was a clear space with a polished wooden floor at the back, for dancing, I guess. There were music stands, anyway. I knew a band was coming.

Kylie looked up. "I saw the man whose job it is—all day, every day, five days a week—to polish the crystal chandeliers."

Each glittery diamond teardrop caught the light inside and cast it out across the room. It was to die for. Especially now that we knew what it cost someone to keep them sparkling.

"So, should we schedule another family wedding in about ten years?" I teased Kylie. She looked surprised and then blushed. "Ha-ha." Then she changed the subject. I'd noticed she was good at that. This time I'd let her get away with it.

We went to each table—the glass bowls had already been carefully set in the centers—and added the colored glass marbles. I got some water pitchers from the kitchen, and we poured water into each bowl before we snuggled the multi-colored flowers inside each one. We set the poster with the little face flowers on an easel, where they could smile upon the dance floor. On the way out we stopped in the room alongside the ballroom where the wedding ceremony itself would take place.

The floor was jade; the room was cool. A huge dome was in the center of the ceiling. The wedding planner was setting up the chuppah as we walked in. The guest chairs were all neatly lined up, patiently waiting in front of the platform the rabbi would speak from.

But would there be a rabbi?

"Want to see something cool?" the wedding planner asked me as Kylie ran back into the room to check the glass bowls one last time.

I nodded.

"Go into the far corner of the room," she said.

She stood in the center, right under the dome, and whispered, "Secrets can't be kept in this room."

Even though I was very far away from her, almost out the door, in fact, I'd heard every whispered word.

I wondered if *my* secrets could be kept in this room.

"Awesome! How did you do that?" I asked.

"The dome reflects sound," she told me. "It's something almost no one knows about the hotel."

I checked my watch. "Oh no! My dad has arranged a Mother's Day present for us, so I'd better get going."

Kylie arrived from the ballroom. "I'm going to help Leeann get dressed and then get myself ready."

"Let's meet at your room one hour before the service," I said. "I'll do your hair, and then we can put the daisy chains around the tables and over the chuppah."

We agreed and took the elevator back upstairs.

When I got into the room, my mom and Bubbie were already waiting. "I thought maybe you'd been overcome by pollen with all the flowers," my mother said, checking her watch.

"Ma, I'm five minutes late," I said.

"Let's go," Dad said. He steered the three of us into the elevator, and we took it downstairs to the lowest level.

"Where are we going?" my mother asked. She had her answer when we stopped in front of the salon.

"I arranged for you to have someone do your hair professionally," Daddy said. He held up his hand. "Not that you don't do a beautiful job on your own—heaven help the man brave enough to suggest that. I just thought it would be a nice treat."

My mom leaned over and kissed one cheek, and I kissed the other. Bubbie grinned. "I could use a little pampering."

I'd already washed my hair today. I didn't want to tell

Dad, though, since he'd gone to so much trouble.

Three different stylists took us separately to do our hair. I could hear Bubbie explaining just how her hair needed to be done to a patient young woman who obviously had a grandmother of her own.

My stylist—André—brushed out my hair and gave me a dreamy scalp massage. "I think you missed a spot," I told him, trying to stretch out the pleasure. He laughed. "I don't think so," he said. "And we have quite a lot to do."

I caught my mother smiling at a station nearby. She winked at me in the mirror and I winked back.

André started pulling back sections of my hair and pinning it up.

"Excuse me, I'm sorry, what are we doing?" I asked as politely as possible.

"An updo," he said. "French twist with curly tendrils."

I looked in the mirror. Boo-hoo! I was already starting to look so good, and now I was going to have to tell him to take it down. As I readied myself to speak up, André handed a note to me. It was on the hotel stationery.

I opened it up and read. "Dearest Rachel, I realize I have been holding you back too much when you've done everything in a trustworthy manner. It's time you had a lovely young woman's hairdo for a special event. I love you. Dad."

Tears filled my eyes. Dad had arranged for this, for me. And I did not deserve it. If only he knew about the

Yacht Club and the tiny fingers I felt pulling me to at least investigate Yeshua—aka Jesus.

I blinked away the tears and smiled as I remembered another thing from that newspaper article I'd seen at Bubbie's. Teens need a new and unusual hairstyle. I looked at mine. There you go.

When we went upstairs, Daddy had already left—he was going to help his brother, Uncle Sid. I wanted to thank Dad—and to talk with him about the summer job. I just couldn't wait any longer. I should have done it sooner, like Ellen had said. Now I'd have no chance before the wedding, and, really, I didn't want to spoil things for him right now. It would have to wait a few hours.

I got into my dress and put my ruby earrings in, and then I left the room to Bubbie so she could get ready, too.

I called Kylie, and we met at her room so I could do her hair before we went downstairs.

"You look fabulous," she said. "But I thought you weren't supposed to twist your hair back?"

"My dad arranged for it," I said. "He thought I should have it because I'm being trustworthy."

Kylie sat down in front of me, and I braided her hair and pinned it up while she talked. "You don't seem too happy."

I told her the *truth* about my summer job.

She nodded. "I understand, I really do."

"I know you do," I said. "I remember about your camp."

I finished up her braid and slipped the crystal stars into her hair while she put twinkling earrings in each ear lobe. "Now *you* look beautiful," I told her. "My brother will be completely taken with you."

"Yeah," she said quietly. "Okay, let's go!"

We gently carried the daisy chains out to the chuppah and lined them over each side. Then we took the little daisy chain rings we'd made and circled the glass bowls on the tables. Finally, we laid a chain down on each side of the aisle that Davina would walk down. We had already given Aunt Beth the bridal bouquet. We were set.

Fifteen minutes before the ceremony was to begin, people began filtering in and sitting down in chairs. Aunt Beth introduced the rabbi to Uncle Sid and Aunt Momo. He was definitely Jewish. But he was the rabbi at Davina's Messianic congregation, so he was Christian, too. A *Christian* rabbi! What would Zayde have thought?

I noticed a nice-looking teenage boy next to him helping to arrange things at the front. He looked like the rabbi's son. I patted my hair to make sure it was still in place. I noticed him looking at me out of the corner of his eye. Again. And again.

I smiled. He did, too.

It was past sundown—so it wasn't officially Sabbath anymore—five minutes before the ceremony was about to begin, and almost every chair on both sides of the aisle was settled. The best man was waiting. Davina and Uncle Sid were waiting in the hallway. The musicians were poised.

A few minutes later Jed walked in, smoothing his hair. He stood at the front and the wedding march began. We all stood and looked toward the back of the room, where Uncle Sid was bringing Davina down the aisle. She seemed to move forward without walking—graceful and soft, like sea-foam advancing on a beach. Her creamy dress clung to her tan skin, her long hair was all around her shoulders, and she had on a dia-mond teardrop necklace that I knew had been Bubbie's. She looked at the daisy chains around her and smiled. I looked back at Kylie, who winked at me. Davina entered the chuppah and walked around Jed, as was our Jewish tradition. Uncle Sid melted away and went to sit with Aunt Momo. My mother and Bubbie were already crying. I was torn between being terribly touched and sneaking glances at the rabbi's son.

As Davina got under the chuppah, Jed lifted the daisy chain we'd made of the tiniest daisies onto her head as a tiara.

The crowd sighed.

"Ruchel," Bubbie said under her breath.

"What?" I whispered back. She blinked and shook her head. "Nu. Davina."

I understood. She wasn't whispering to me. She was

thinking about how very much like Davina *her* Rachel would have looked.

Normally the rabbi would begin his talk at this point. Instead, Jed spoke up. "I have a surprise for Davina, a gift and a promise to begin our married life together." He plucked one of the daisies out of her bouquet. "I know that life has not been easy for Davina in the past few years."

I wondered if he meant when her other fiancé jilted her or how hard it had been on her to reconcile her new faith with her family.

"But she will never have to walk through anything alone again. She loves daisies, so I have made sure there are plenty here, with help from some wedding elves."

I beamed, so glad to be able to help.

"Here is my promise to you." He held up the single daisy and plucked a petal. "I love you." He plucked another and another. "I love you, and I love you. I will never love you not."

He continued plucking petals, and Bubbie was letting the tears stream now. My mother handed over a hanky but kept one for herself.

"I'm quoting a passage that Davina and I love, said to us about another kind of love, but repeated by me, here, to her.

"I am convinced that nothing can ever separate us." He plucked a petal off with each declaration.

DAISY CHAINS

"Death can't. Life can't. The angels can't, and the demons can't. Our fears for today, our worries about tomorrow, and even the powers of hell can't keep my love away. Whether we are high above the sky or in the deepest ocean, nothing in all creation will ever be able to separate us."

Davina's face streamed with tears while Jed completed picking off all the petals till they formed a confetti of love at her feet, ending each with "I love you."

The rabbi drew us together and performed the service. At the end, Jed stomped on a crystal glass, shattering it in dozens of pieces. That is a promise that just as those pieces can't be put together again, so the marriage can never be taken apart.

That was always the best part of a wedding, to me.

Bubbie whispered to me, "Zayde used to say that's the last time the man will ever be able to put his foot down." I chuckled with her, oh so glad that she was there.

Uncle Sid stood and shouted, *"Mazel tov!"* And we all joined him and clapped.

We went forward to greet and celebrate with the couple, moving into the ballroom. Jed and Davina stood at the head of the line, greeting everyone. Kylie's uncle Andy and aunt Beth and my uncle Sid and aunt Momo were also there. Bubbie stood at the end—the most important place, after all, finishing the greeting line with a grand flourish.

The food was delicious. Lightly poached chicken breasts with a creamy sauce, and the thinnest green beans I'd ever seen, sweating garlic butter. The cake was a beautiful confection of the season's first hot-house strawberries and cream. When the band struck up a few notes, I saw who was one of the first on the floor. My brother—*my* brother—danced a hip-hop dance with Kylie, who looked pretty as always.

The rabbi's son, Sam, asked me to dance. Of course I obliged him, thanking God for sending a one-night dance partner my way so I didn't feel like Jake's kid sister. I danced with my dad, too. But then Sam asked again, and again.

Heh-heh. Maybe they didn't *all* like blondes.

"Thanks for the hairdo, Daddy," I said at my second dance with him. "I ... I've been meaning to talk with you about something."

He must have caught the concerned look on my face. He put his finger to his lips. "Shush, not tonight. All is right now. We can talk later, but tonight, we enjoy."

I saw Kylie, looking at me with my dad. She turned away before she could catch my eye. I know she was thinking of her very absent dad. I drew closer to my own.

Davina came by and hugged me. "Thank you for doing the daisy chains. I know how long that must have taken you guys. You know I love daisies, but to me, the chains of daisies mean so much more. It means all of us, holding hands as friends and family no matter what happens. It shows me the connectedness of my Jewish faith with my belief in Jesus."

I hugged her back, and she went off to dance with my dad.

I saw Kylie and my brother leave the room to talk in the atrium, the room next door with a glass ceiling so the stars shone through. Jake looked so happy! But when they came back, even though Kylie was wearing Jake's suit coat to guard her bare arms against the chilly night, Jake looked very sad indeed. Not at all like the jitterbug who'd cut up the dance floor an hour ago.

What had happened between them? Could it be fixed?

Jed and Davina had taken off in a horse-drawn carriage for a moonlit ride. The guests started to leave then, drifting from the ballroom into the wedding chamber on the way back to their rooms. I stood by the door talking with Bubbie. "I noticed you danced with the groom," I teased.

"Yes. Well, if a man comes and trims back my yard and cuts back my trees and takes care of my garden the week before his wedding, and all he asks in return is a wedding dance, well, who am I to turn down a bargain?"

Jed had cared for Bubbie's garden.

Jake walked Bubbie up to bed, and I hung out by the door, waiting to talk with Kylie. She stood in the center of the room, under the dome, talking with my mom. I smiled. They didn't know I could hear them. Heh-heh.

My mother said something about having matzo bread and nothing else for breakfast after such a rich dinner.

"Oh yes," Kylie answered in perfect deadly innocence. "I know what matzo is. Davina told us all about it when she taught Rachel and me how very Christian the Passover really is." I saw her mouth slow down as she realized she perhaps shouldn't have brought that up.

I watched my mother's eyes fly open in horror, though she'd never say anything to Kylie. I, for one, was going to hear the rest of Kylie's story another night. I left the room as quickly as possible. Could I make it to my room before my mom got to me and demanded some answers about why I was learning about a "Christian" Passover? She wouldn't wake Bubbie's sleep by knocking on the door.

Mayday! Mayday! I ran for it before Mom could disentangle herself from the guests.

CHAPTER NINE
kylie's story

Jacob's Coat *Acalypha wilkesiana*
A beautiful plant grown for its copper leaves with white tips—almost resembling an arrow. It's a tender perennial. Treat with care.
—Northwest Gardener's Guide

Jacob's coat was settled gently with a stack of books in a corner of my room; I was unwilling but required to return it!
—Kylie Peterson

I ran into the house after school on Wednesday and got it all cleaned up. Tonight Mom and I were going out—alone—to celebrate Mother's Day, since I'd missed it last Sunday when I was at the wedding.

I loaded and started the dishwasher and ran the vacuum so she wouldn't have to worry about it—and because I wanted to—and helped Hayley with her homework. "That way you can have a good time with Mary and not worry about it."

"I wouldn't worry about it either way," Hayley said. I smiled. That was one difference between Hayley and me.

Maybe I could learn a thing or two from her.

"I made dinner reservations somewhere really special," Mom said. "At an Italian restaurant in Ballard." We hardly ever went into Seattle for dinner. We had plenty of good places here in Issaquah. But going "in town" was a treat, too.

"Do you feel bad paying for your own Mother's Day dinner?" I asked. "I did get those Victoria Creams, remember. And I cleaned the house."

"I don't mind paying, honey, and I have been eating a cream a day since Sunday. You can pay for dinner sometime this summer when *you're* making more money and *I'm* making *less*," she said.

I looked up and she put her finger to her lips. "We'll talk more about that at dinner." We enjoyed the rain pattering on the windshield and talked about my day at school and the classes I wanted to sign up for next year—high school! Ninth grade! But I was so curious about what she meant about the money. And I hadn't shared my big news with her. I'd waited for a special occasion. Tonight.

Once seated at a little corner table with a starched white tablecloth, we ordered an appetizer of sautéed mushrooms and a spicy Caesar salad. Mom said, "I can see you have something to say. You go first."

"How did you know?" I asked, shocked, tearing off a spongy piece of bread from the basket.

"Because I'm the mom, that's why." She smiled and popped a piece of bread into her own mouth.

"Well, you know how I've been really interested in church things and stuff lately?" I started.

She nodded.

"Well, I've kind of realized that I never really was a Christian."

Mom stopped chewing. "What do you mean?"

I cleared my throat and explained what I'd learned at church and with Davina and by watching Sarah and those Bible verses. "Being a Christian is not something you just fall into. You need to choose it."

She nodded slowly but kind of sideways, and she didn't look entirely convinced but instead a little nervous. I knew how she felt. I'd felt that same way.

"Well, anyway, I prayed about it one night and

decided I really truly did want to, you know, be a Christian. So now I am."

My mom smiled. "If that makes you happy, it makes me happy."

"I feel happy—and . . . I don't know, *right*. Have you noticed?"

She genuinely smiled. "I think I actually have."

"I'd also like to go to church more," I said. "Sarah's church, because, you know, Grandpa doesn't really go very often. Plus I kind of want to go where Sarah is, and the camp people."

"We can stop in there every once in a while," Mom said. She nodded at the waiter, who had just brought our salad. "Thank you," she said as he ground some pepper on it.

"I'd like to go a lot more," I said. "Like maybe every week. Hayley liked it, too." Now I was reaching, dragging Hayley into it to get my way. *Ay-yi-yi*.

Mom took a few bites and swallowed. "Grandpa might be hurt that you don't like his church anymore. And you *know* how he feels about religious nuts." She quickly added, "Not that that is what you are!"

I took a bite of my salad and used my most respectful tone. "I know that's what *he* thinks, Mom. But is it okay with *you*?"

There was a long silence. The waiter refilled our bread and poured more water into the glasses, ice clinking, water tumbling, lemon slice bobbing like a sail.

"You're right, Kylie," Mom said finally. "I guess those are *his* words and thoughts, not mine. I . . . I don't know if I'll be going every week, but if Sarah will take you when I can't . . ."

"I'm sure she will," I said, not showing, I hoped, that I was a little sad. I guess I had hoped she'd be excited to come, too. Hayley was. Mom had seemed to like it.

We ordered our pasta—Mom's with duck sauce and mine with truffles—and the waiter left again. "Well, here's the thing. I need to tell the camp staff that I really just officially became a Christian. Because the rules are that you need to be a Christian for at least one year. So they might not let me be a counselor." I took a sip of water. "It was a misunderstanding to start with. But now it's not. And I don't want to lie."

My eyes welled up a bit. "Gramps will be so disappointed in me."

Mom took a sip of her lemon water. "How do *you* feel about it?" she finally asked, reflecting my own words back on me.

"Good." I grinned. "Scared, but right." I told her about my sharing my colored water and flower lesson this coming Sunday, and she smiled. "That's really good, Kyls."

Our pasta came, and Mom talked to me in more detail about the past weekend she and Hayley had enjoyed. "We baked a cake—that failed—and then ran to a bakery to get a ready-made one, which we nibbled at all weekend. We went for a ride in that convertible, of course. Hayley told you all about it—"

"A convertible!" I said. "I still can't believe it. Without me."

Mom laughed out loud. "I wrote some freelance ad copy for a car dealer, and they let me use one for the day. Hayley has always wanted to ride in a convertible. She had a ball."

"I noticed she hasn't used a brace or a sling or her inhaler all week."

Mom nodded. "She needs me around more. Kylie, I'm thinking of changing jobs. I've had a headhunter looking for jobs for me for the past few months, and he thinks he's found something."

"Oh! *That* kind of headhunter." I remembered Hayley's comment about a tribal headhunter some weeks ago over her poached eggs.

"It'd mean leaving the security—and prestige— of the downtown ad firm. I'd only be working sixty percent of the time, so I'd have to do freelance work like I did for the dealership the rest of the time. I'd have to find some other clients on my own."

"Would we have enough to live on?" I asked in a small voice.

"Probably. I haven't been willing to take any, you know, risks since your dad and I split," she said. "But I'm worn out. And you girls are, too."

I didn't disagree. "Would you be home more often?"

She nodded. "Yes. I'd be working about twenty-five hours a week at an office in Bellevue, only ten minutes from home, but the rest of the work would be at my home office. We'd be living, I guess, by faith, since my freelance wouldn't be steady for a while." She laughed. "I guess we'd have to live by *your* faith since you're the only one in the family that has any."

She sounded shaky, but the years had fallen away from her face. Those two deep creases in her forehead were gone tonight, like water gently brushed over clay, and her green eyes sparkled.

"When do you let them know?" I asked.

"I have to drop off the copy at the dealership Sunday morning. If they offer me another freelance job, I'll take it and assume that's a sign that I should go forward." She winked at me.

Sunday. I'd hoped she could go with me to church. *Oh well.* Sarah could take me.

My phone rang, and the people at the next table looked at me. How embarrassing that I'd forgotten to turn it off! My mom frowned, and I quick looked at the number before turning it off.

"Jake," I said out loud, distracted.

Tough-as-nails Mom was back. "*That* we will talk about when we get home."

We split a tiramisu for dessert and play-fought over the radio station all the way home—Mom wanting to listen to eighties music, and me? Hip-hop, of course. *Clean* hip-hop. The whole night was great. Almost as good as Sarah's family, but kinda better, 'cause it was *my* family.

When I got home, Mom let me return Jake's call. His voice was very cool and unemotional, and I guess I shouldn't have expected any different after what we'd talked about on Saturday night. I'd had to tell him that, well, that I wasn't allowed to have a boyfriend. That he was starting to seem more than a friend to me. In fact maybe always had. That it was against my mom's rules, and even though I wanted things to stay the same, they just couldn't.

He seemed kind of normal to me on the boat on the way back to Seattle, though, so I thought everything had been okay. I guess that had been for the benefit of the others around us.

I sighed and dialed. "Hi, Jake," I said when he answered. "Sorry I couldn't answer your call earlier; I was at dinner with my mom."

"You don't have to let me know where you were," he said. "I'm working, and I just wondered if

I could stop by afterward and pick up my suit coat and my books."

They were sitting, neatly, in a corner in my bedroom. I'd meant to give him back his coat on Sunday, but it had been a bit of a rush getting out of the hotel. It would have been awkward, too.

"Your sister is coming to church with me on Sunday," I said. "So if you don't want to pick them up tonight, she can get them then and bring them back."

I heard him inhale sharply, but he said nothing. "Nah, I'll swing by," he said. I think he really secretly wanted to come, but I said nothing.

My mom stopped by my door as soon as she heard the phone flip shut.

"You know, my rule about no boyfriends till you're older is for your own good," she said. "Anything that's right for you is right for me. But no boyfriend for now."

"How do you know I was starting to think of him as a boyfriend?" I demanded. "You haven't been around enough to notice."

Sting. She flinched.

"I'm sorry, Mom. I'm sorry." I walked over to her and she hugged me.

"I'm the mom, that's why. And I notice more than you think."

"I know," I said into the fold of her hug, not wanting it to end just yet. "It's been a hard week."

She looked over my shoulder at the bulletin board—with Jake's email address on it. Yikes! Instead, she took the article I'd cut out those weeks ago about how teens need independence. "I see the ones you've checked," she said.

I nodded, a little embarrassed. "I kinda want to do teen things," I said.

She nodded and pinned it back to the board. "I can't blame you." She walked out of my room with her mind obviously a hundred miles away. I gathered Jake's stuff in a Safeway bag, except for his coat, which I'd kept on a plastic hanger. I set aside the *Northwest Gardener's Guide* Aunt Beth had given me to plan for the wedding. I'd kind of liked looking up flowers and stuff. I could see why she enjoyed it. I really should return that, too.

Half an hour later the doorbell rang. It was Jake.

"Hi," I said. I had the bag and the coat right next to me.

"Hi," he said. He still had that cute baseball hat on.

"You still look like DJ Jazzy Jake," I said.

He grinned but not for long. "I'd probably better get going. My parents are expecting me."

I handed the stuff over to him. I wasn't going to say anything cheesy like "Can we be friends," because I didn't really feel ready to be friends with him yet. The wound in my heart was too tender, and the temptation to disobey my mom was still strong.

He didn't look like he was in any big hurry to be friends with me, either.

"Okay. Maybe I'll see you at Davina and Jed's party in June," I said. They were going to have a big party at Aunt Beth and Uncle Andy's at the end of the month, when their wedding was supposed to have taken place before the Empress freed up. Everyone who couldn't come to Victoria, and even the people who could, was supposed to come over for a barbecue.

"I'm working a lot this summer," Jake said.

"Maybe I'll see you on Sunday if you drive Rachel over," I said.

"Maybe. Well, good to see you," he said a bit more softly. Even though he was mad and hurt, he couldn't hide his real character from me, which was kind.

"You too," I said. I went into the house and closed the door behind me. I felt sad. But right.

I went into my room and booted up the computer. I sent an email to Rachel. We hadn't really talked to each other since the wedding. It had taken up so much of our lives for so long that we had a lot of real life to catch up on. It was almost the end of the school year, and we both had a lot to do.

Hey Ray,

*I'm looking forward to you coming on Sunday. Can
you get here about 8:40 or so? Sarah will be here about
8:45 to get us, and we can drive you home afterward if
Jake can't come and get you. I'm so glad you're coming.*

*I've missed you! We need to plan our next get-
together. Shopping?*

Daisies forever,
Kylie

Then I called Sarah. Her voice mail was on.
"Hey, I'm looking forward to Sunday. My friend
Rachel is coming, too. Isn't that cool? I hope she
likes it. I need to talk with you, though, about my,
um, talk, or whatever you call it. So call me, okay?
I'd better leave a message for Ben at the church and
tell him that what I'm going to say is a little different. I hope that's okay. You said it was supposed to
be what was happening with God in my life, and
when I became a Christian. Well, that's what it's
going to be. Call me, okay? I want to tell you first."

I hung up and left a message for Ben on his
voice mail at church saying kind of the same thing.
Then I finished my homework, distracted.

Surely when they saw that the lesson was really
good they'd see I'd be a good camp counselor, too.
Did I tell them about the time I helped with Hayley's
ballet class? I don't know. I'd have to remember to
tell them that. Honesty counted for something,
right?

"All of those things count, right?" I asked Missy. "I'll get to keep the job, right?" I waved her treat up and down, and she nodded her agreement before gobbling the treat and snuggling at the foot of my bed.

I crawled into bed. *Please, God. Now I really* do *have something to share with those kids. Please let me keep that job.*

CHAPTER TEN
rachel's story

Herb of Repentance; Herb of Grace *Ruta graveolens L*
Small perennial herb bush with soft gray leaves and yellow cup-like flowers historically thought to ward off the Black Death. An ancient remedy against, among other things, nose bleeds, high blood pressure, and trauma.

—Northwest Gardener's Guide

Growing up means doing the hard things and taking responsibility before asking for more freedom. I had the herb of repentance to offer my father. I was not at all sure that he would offer me the self-same herb of grace in return.

—Rachel Cohen

"I'm late!" I told Jake. "I told you we should have left earlier!"

"Well, *excuse* me," he said. "I'm not your personal chauffeur service. I had to work this morning. And in case I need to remind you, this is positively more than the ten trips I promised I'd take you on. The next one costs you two dollars."

"Will you take me to Kylie's house tomorrow morning?"

"Nope."

"For two dollars?"

"Nope."

Kylie was an off-limits topic since we'd come back from the wedding last week.

He screeched to a stop in front of the Yacht Club. The parking lot was packed—a sunny Saturday afternoon in mid-May, and people were starting to get into the swing of warmer weather.

"I'll be back in ten minutes. Then we'll be a little early for clarinet lessons, but you can drop me off and I'll just wait."

"Okay. Mom'll pick you up from the lesson and take you home before she and I leave for the movie tonight. After *Dad* comes home," he said with a menacing tone.

He'd obviously noticed the tension at home and thought I was going to get it bad.

He sat in his truck in the parking lot as I ran inside the club. I snatched my waiting guest pass at the front desk and followed the yellow arrows back to the training room.

Oh no. Class had already started. Joanie smiled at me, friendly-like, and I gave her a sickly half grin. Melissa waved and patted a chair right between her and Ellen. I slipped into it and then sat there stewing in my own anxious juices.

This was obviously going to take more than ten minutes. Jake was going to kill me, but I couldn't interrupt the class any further.

They went over the safety regulations, the etiquette expected of Yacht Club employees, and the fact that there were no benefits. No benefits! Well, of course. We were kids.

"Everything okay?" Ellen leaned over and whispered.

I shook my head no. She wasn't expecting that but reached over and squeezed my arm anyway.

Joanie droned on and on and then led us into the locker room. Because I couldn't very well interrupt her in the middle of the class, I just stayed silent.

"I'll talk with you afterward," I whispered to Melissa, on my other side. She nodded, concerned.

Joanie finished up, and as she did, I drew Melissa aside. "Come over here for a sec."

"Where's your swim bag? We're going to hang out afterward."

I drew her to the nearby bench, next to a slightly smelly bucket of used towels.

"I can't work with you guys this summer. I came here today to tell Joanie in person."

"Why *not*?"

"I didn't get my parents' permission before signing up. I . . . I'm really sorry about that," I said. "I wanted to be with you guys so much, and I didn't want you to think my dad was a hard case or anything."

"I'm so sorry he said no," Melissa said. "Would it help if my dad talked to him?"

I shook my head. "The thing is, even though he didn't officially say no, I knew what his feelings were about the whole thing. It's just the right thing to do. See, I've been doing all these things and then expecting my parents to say okay later. I hate it when they make decisions for my life and then tell me about them later. I guess I don't want to do the same thing to them."

Melissa held on to my arm. "Don't tell Joanie yet. If you do she'll give the job away to someone else. Talk with your dad first."

"I can't," I said. "I thought about it all week, which is why I haven't said anything. I want to do it so bad. But I've been doing that too much—acting first and then telling him later. I'm so sorry."

My eye caught the bulletin board with the rundown of the summer fun list.

I read them over again and sighed.

• Weekly Bonfires—we supply the marshmallows and

chocolate, you supply your voice and sense of fun!
- Pontoon Parties—What Floats Your Boat? Come and find out. Anyone aged 13–17 welcome.
- Shipwreck Party—Are You Down With It? We are. Sign-ups start Memorial Day. See the front desk.

"I'm sorry for you, too," Melissa said. "With me and Carmel and Ellen here all summer, what will you do?"

"I don't know." Visions of a summer filled playing bridge with Bubbie and her friends drifted through my mind. Trimming my toenails. Helping my mother clean out the refrigerator. Learning aerobics by myself from a DVD filled with middle-aged women who had had plastic surgery.

I sighed again. Melissa squeezed my hand and walked back to Carmel.

Ellen came up behind me. "Everything okay?"

I nodded and was about to tell her, too, when Joanie came up to us. "Do you want me to leave?" Ellen whispered.

I shook my head. I'd rather have her there. "May I please speak with you?" I asked Joanie.

"Sure, kiddo." Joanie slipped the pen through the top of her clipboard.

"I'm sorry if this is a problem for you, but I won't be able to take the job this summer," I said. "I . . . I didn't really have my parents' permission before I said yes."

"Oh, sorry to hear that," she said. "You sure?"

I drew myself up to my full five feet two inches. "Yes. I'm sure."

"Okey-dokey. It's no worry to me, hon; I'll be able to get your position filled like that." She snapped her fingers and started walking forward. "I appreciate that you came and told me in person. And that you told me the truth and didn't offer me some lame excuse. Shows real character and maturity." She nodded, snapped her gum, and moved on.

Ellen came and sat on the bench with me.

"I wish I had listened to you and talked with my dad sooner," I said.

Ellen smiled softly. "Yeah. No swim bag? No bon voyage swim?"

"Jake's waiting outside to take me to clarinet lessons."

"Still going through with *that* plan, then, eh?" Ellen asked.

"Yes. If Mrs. Rosenthal agrees." I forced a smile. "My dad comes home tonight."

"Whatcha going to do all summer?" Ellen asked.

"Eat Spanish peanuts and play cards with old ladies," I joked. "Clean my CDs. Learn how to count backward in Spanish."

She laughed with me. "There. My best friend is poking her head out from the clouds again."

"I'd better get going," I said.

"Call me when you get home from clarinet," Ellen

said. "Let me know how it goes."

She hugged me, and I hugged her back.

On the way out I kicked the bucket of towels and caught a whiff—sweaty, steamy from the room, and pungent from the pool chemicals.

I hated to admit it, because it sounded so much worse for me if everything about this job I had just given up had been perfect, but I felt a slight tingle of relief. I hated cleaning. Really. Why would I have wanted a summer job cleaning?

To be with your friends and make some money.

Oh yeah.

I headed out to the parking lot, where the little silver truck sat waiting. Jake closed his book as soon as I opened the car door. I noticed it was science fiction—not medieval literature.

"That was short and sweet. *Not!*" he said. "What was that all about?"

I wanted Jake to see me as the young woman I was becoming, too. "I accepted a job without mom and dad's permission. So I just quit."

He stepped on the gas and we pulled forward. "Does Dad know about it now?"

"No. I'll tell him tonight."

I promised myself I would not do this again. *Mental note: Make dad's favorite dessert for our coffee time tonight—chocolate chip cookies.*

Jake was silent till we pulled up at Mrs. Rosenthal's

house. "Does Dad know you're going to church with Kylie on Sunday?"

"How did *you* know that's where we're going?"

He shrugged. He was like the sea—he gave up no secrets. "Well?"

I shook my head. "No. He doesn't. Yet."

There it was again. That same look. He obviously thought I was going to get it bad.

"Mom will be here to pick you up after your lesson," he said. "Good luck," he added softly, then reached over and hugged me. I don't know why the tears came forward then, but they did, and I didn't let go of the hug as quickly as I might have.

I sniffed and wiped my eyes with the back of my hand. "Thanks, Jakey." I grabbed my clarinet case and music folder and then walked into Mrs. Rosenthal's studio.

"So, we're back to Saturdays now that the big wedding is over?" She sat on one of the lesson chairs and I sat next to her. "That is, for one more month till school is out, and then you're done?"

I opened my case and began screwing together my clarinet. "Well, I wanted to talk with you about that." I tightened the pieces and made sure my reed wasn't chipped. "How much money would it be for my dad and me to take summer lessons together?"

I wouldn't sign up for anything without Dad's permission, but there was no harm in getting information, right?

Mrs. Rosenthal pretended to do some calculations, but the gleam in her eye and the smile on her face gave her away. "You know, it's your lucky week."

If she only knew how *un*lucky this week was.

"I have just decided to give two-for-one lessons for the summer if it's a father and a daughter. Assuming the daughter will continue as my student the next school year. Kind of—" she searched for the word—"an incentive plan!"

I smiled. "Thank you. I'll talk with my dad about it tonight," I said. "Do you have a duet book handy?"

"Let's work on this lesson, and if Yitzhak is interested, I will find a duet book somewhere in the studio. Or I'll order it on the Internet. I'm computer savvy." She beamed with pride.

I held back a smile, wet the rough bamboo of my reed, and began my warm-up scales.

Right on time, my mother pulled up in front to get me. I took apart my clarinet while Mrs. Rosenthal peeled off a foil star and put it on my lesson page.

I wonder if she'll do that for Dad's pages? I thought, amused. *Probably.*

"I am glad you're not quitting clarinet and that your father was able to talk some sense into you."

"My father doesn't know yet," I said. "But if he allows me to continue, I will."

"Why did you want to quit, anyway? You have such talent."

To be with my friends, I thought. *To be someone different*. All I said was, "To do something different."

"Doing different for the sake of doing different is nothing smart at all," Mrs. Rosenthal said. "Unless it's something you yourself want to do."

"I know that now." I'd forgotten how much I loved playing clarinet.

When I got to the car, my mom leaned over and opened the door for me. "Everything go okay?"

I nodded. "Can we stop at the store on the way home? I'd like to make some chocolate chip cookies for Dad and me when we have our coffee tonight."

My mother nodded. We were going to eat dinner together as a family, and then she'd planned for her and Jake to be away from the house while I talked with my dad.

I hadn't seen him since the wedding night, since he'd left very early Sunday morning for his convention and was only flying back home tonight.

"Thank you for letting me go today," I said.

"You're welcome. It hasn't been an easy week, and it's not going to get any easier tonight." She kissed me on the cheek. "But I know you can do it."

"Are you still mad at me?"

She shook her head. "Mad? Not anymore. Sad? A little, still. I wish you had talked to me when you first had questions about your faith. Love you? Always."

"Have you said anything to Daddy?" I'd already had to give Mom full disclosure.

"I told you I'd let you talk with him on your own, and I kept his best interests in mind, too," Mom continued. "I didn't want him worried and preoccupied on his trip. It was nothing that couldn't wait a few days." She smoothed her hair back. "Although it might have been easier if I'd cushioned the blow a little ahead of time."

"Thank you, Mom," I said.

We walked through Quality Food Center and picked out the things for the cookies. I tossed them into the car and we drove home together, my mother and I, talking too much about almost nothing in order to fill the air space and make the tension melt away.

It never worked.

My dad's plane was supposed to arrive at about four in the afternoon. At three o'clock my mom checked the airline schedule, and it looked like it might be a little late.

"I'll make the cookies now!" I announced in a spirit of fake confidence.

I pulled all of the ingredients out on the counter and lined them up. Normally I would have just yanked them out of the cupboard one by one when I needed to use them, and then I'd come across something strange in the recipe, like baking powder, and see that the can was practically empty, and then I'd try to substitute something else. And then the recipe would fail.

However, the new and improved Rachel made lists. She did things in an organized way. Her ideas were mature and well thought out and certain to be a success.

Or so I hoped.

After mixing everything together, I put the dough into the fridge to chill.

At five o'clock the arrival schedule said my dad's plane would be in at six. "We'll have to eat without him," my mother said.

I kept the dough in the fridge. I planned to bake the cookies at six-thirty so they'd be warm and fresh when we ate them. I was leaving nothing to chance, however. "Mom, will you make the coffee before you leave?"

Smart girls know when to ask for help.

We popped a frozen pizza into the oven, and my mother sliced up cucumbers and set them on the green flowered dishes we used in the spring and the summer. She ate her pizza with a fork and a knife. In the interest of my new, mature, ladylike behavior, I followed her example.

Jake just stared before picking up his piece like a Neanderthal.

"I'll just have time to get Daddy and drop him off and pick up Jake before we'll need to race to the movies," Mom said. I cleared the table while she programmed the coffeepot.

Jake went into his room; I could hear him talking

on the phone. I preheated the oven. Mom went to pick up Dad.

I'd read somewhere that if you scoop out cookie dough with an ice cream scoop they all come out in perfectly uniform sizes and shapes, and then nothing underbakes or overbakes.

I dug around the utensil drawer for the ice cream scoop and finally found it entangled with a garlic press and a lemon zester. I took the dough out of the refrigerator and let it warm up just a little. I thought that was so weird. Why do they tell you to refrigerate the dough, but then you have to let it soften in order to bake the cookies?

Just as I'd popped the first batch into the oven my dad came into the house. He hugged and kissed Jake before Jake ran out to the car to head to the movies with my mother.

Daddy hugged me. He still had his coat on, and it smelled like aftershave and dry cleaning. His shirt was a bit wrinkly but starchy. He smelled like a dad. I burrowed myself into his arms as I hadn't in a long time.

I'd thought that part of growing up was growing away. Now I wasn't so sure.

"Big plans for us, eh?" Dad said.

I tried to smile, but it came out lopsided, I know, as if I had a mouth full of grapes. If he only knew.

"I'm going to shower, and then we can talk. Mom said you'd like to talk with me." I saw the concern on his face. He was a smart man. He knew something was up. "Where do you want to talk?"

"In the living room?" I said. I had to think it through. Were there any large heavy objects in there that he could throw? The idea of that brought a smile to my lips. My dad was so calm that my mother said she was sometimes unsure if he actually had a pulse.

I, on the other hand, was more like my mother.

Dad went into the shower, and I pulled the first batch of cookies out of the oven. "Oh no!" I tried to scrape them off of the cookie sheet as quickly as possible. The bottoms were tar. Okay, not tar, but definitely a very dark bark.

I grabbed the other sheet; I'd already scooped cookie dough onto it. I set it into the oven and set the timer for five minutes less than the batch I'd just made.

Then I went into my room and brushed my hair. I came back out and turned on the coffee machine and it started percolating.

The cookies were done. I took them out and they looked kind of doughy. Almost every cookie I scraped off wrinkled like a caterpillar. "Great. Sound wave cookies."

Exasperated, I turned the oven off and put the rest of the dough back into the fridge.

Dad came out of his room in jeans and a T-shirt. He looked refreshed. "Something sure smells good!" he said as he walked into the living room.

"It's the coffee," I offered.

"Smells like cookies—chocolate chip, my favorite!"

I set the tray down on the coffee table and sat down beside him. "You even get to make a choice," I said, my voice somewhat exasperated. "Overdone or underdone."

Dad smiled and picked a cookie at random. "They're sure to be especially sweet given the hands that made them. My sister used to be a terrible baker, too," he said, not recognizing the dis.

Thank you, Dad. You just brought up the subject for me.

"Dad, actually, that's kind of what I want to talk with you about." I knew I was supposed to start with what *I* had done wrong and not with what *he* had done wrong, but I needed to start here, I think, at the beginning.

"My sister Rachel?" Dad looked genuinely surprised.

"I feel like I'm living in her shadow. I know you really love me, and that you want to protect me, but I feel like sometimes I have to do everything really safe because you are afraid I'm going to die like she did. So I end up staying like *this*"—I picked up the picture of me in pigtails on the arm table next to the sofa—"in your mind."

I touched his hand. "I'm not a little girl anymore, Dad. Everyone is trying to protect me, but instead I'm suffocating." The hand I was touching flinched, and he rubbed his temples with the other.

A minute or more ticked by on the grandfather clock. I kept watching Dad, even though I really wanted to look down. I forced my head to stay up and meet whatever came head on.

"You're right," Dad finally said. "I have been treating you like a little girl. I'm so sorry. I hope my gift of the hairdo at the wedding shows you that I'm changing. And, Rachel, you're so special, so much your own girl, that you could never live in anyone's shadow. You shine your own light." He sipped his coffee and ate a second cookie—an overbaked one, obviously. I could hear the crunching. "You are trustworthy."

His soft words made the next things even harder to say.

"Dad, I'm really not. But I'd like to be. I need to confess."

Dad's back stiffened some but he nodded slowly. "Yes...?"

"First, I want to tell you some things I did right. I never wore my hair up before you told me I could. When you told me to change clothes, I did. I didn't sneak them behind your back. Even though I was tempted to." *Might as well start with a few points in my favor.*

Dad nodded.

"But one thing I did do behind your back was sign up for a summer job."

He inhaled. "Where?"

"At the Yacht Club. With Ellen and Carmel and Melissa. Their parents had said yes, and I felt left out. So I said I could do it. The job was going to be cleaning up the locker rooms part time, and then I could hang out at the swim club."

"Oh, Rachel," Dad said. "You didn't."

I sighed. "I did, but I went in today and told her I couldn't keep the job."

Dad stood up, walked into the kitchen, and refilled his coffee from the pot. Then he sat back down. "I understand you want a job, but you are too young to be working in a place where I don't know any of the people, among a lot of strangers. I'm sorry, Rachel. I'm disappointed that you signed up for this job, but I'm glad that you quit and that you told me. I wish you had told me sooner. I wish you hadn't gone behind my back."

"I do, too, Dad." I said. "I did try to tell you at the wedding, remember?"

He nodded and sat back down. "Yes, I do."

I sipped my coffee, my hand shaking.

"But I guess I also need to be the kind of father who makes it easy for his daughter to talk with. I'll pay attention to that."

Can we start that new program right now? "Okay, Dad," I said. He stood to get up, thinking it was over. I dug my toes into the carpet. "I have something else to talk about with you."

He sighed and sat back down. "I don't suppose it's your tennis game."

I shook my head. "When I was over at Davina's

house, she was getting ready for Passover. Did you know she still celebrates Passover?"

My dad shook his head. "No, I didn't."

"Kylie was there, and Davina was teaching her about Passover. When she said she was going to show her all the things in Passover that were Christian, I left right away to sit on the couch and read a magazine."

"*Christian* Passover?" My father stood up. I quick looked around for the heavy objects. His pulse was back.

I nodded. "I tried not to listen, Dad, but you know, it's a small apartment. So I couldn't help but overhear. I didn't say anything to you because, well, I don't know. It sounded like it could possibly make sense."

"Did Davina try to make you a Christian?"

I shook my head. "No."

"Good. Then the subject is closed." He caught his breath. "I'm not doing too well with my new plan to listen thoughtfully, am I?" he said more softly.

We both giggled.

"When we were at the hotel, I opened the Bible that was in the drawer. I read a few sentences of the Christian part. I don't know, Daddy. Maybe it could be true; could it be the real thing?"

My dad said nothing for a minute. "I think it's all fool's gold," he finally said. "It might seem like 'the real thing' until you get up close. But then you'll see it's not what it seems. You'll feel bad for looking at it and examining it and for being tricked. And in the meantime, you'll cause a lot of hurt to people along the way." I know he was thinking of Bubbie, but I didn't bring her up.

I inhaled. *Be bold*, I told myself, remembering my promise to myself. "You might be right. It might be fool's gold. Or it might be the pot of gold at the end of the Jewish rainbow. I don't really know. I'm just saying, if I don't get up close, like you said, and examine it, how will I know for sure?"

Dad sat there, breathing with a "why me?" look on his face. "I don't know. I just don't know." I thought I heard him muttering something about owing Uncle Sid a problem or two.

Dad got up for a third cup of coffee and then came back from the kitchen. "Here's what I want you to know. I will listen carefully to what you say. I will try to give you more freedom. We'll get you a summer job of some sort—maybe with Uncle Sid."

Okay. I didn't really want to swelter with Uncle Sid in his dry cleaning business, but I'd let this go for now.

Dad continued. "I guess you can read up a little on some of this Christian stuff, as long as it doesn't go crazy. *But*—you must come and talk with me about *everything* you read or hear so I can help you see what's fool's gold. You have to be honest with me in all areas of your life. I'm giving you freedom I never had as a boy. I expect you to treat me with respect and open-ness in return." He grinned. "And I promise to try not to burst a blood vessel when we talk."

I hugged him. "I promise, Dad. We'll talk about everything. In ... in some ways, I'm glad Mom heard Kylie talk about the Passover, because I might not have had the courage to bring it up otherwise." I tucked my hair behind my ears. "What will Bubbie think?" I finished in a small voice.

Rachel! I told myself. *You weren't going to say anything!*

"It doesn't matter what *she* thinks as much as what your mother and *I* think." He seemed to be telling himself that as much as me. I think he might have meant that for the very first time.

"No going to any church or doing churchy things," Dad finished. "I'm willing to let you read and talk. But I'm not having you go to Christian places. No talking about things like Christian Passover or other nonsense without talking with your mother and me about it."

It seemed reasonable.

"I promise," I said. "And, Dad, I have one more thing."

"One *more* thing? What else can there possibly be? I've had as much as a man can take in one night! Let's call it quits while I can still stand."

I held up a finger to indicate "Wait a minute," then ran into my room and got both of our clarinets. "I would like us to take lessons together this summer," I said when I returned.

"I thought you were quitting. Is this another bribe to

soothe the angry beast, like the chocolate chip cookies?" he teased.

I giggled. "No. I just realized that, well, I like clarinet.
I wanted to quit kind of to just ... I don't know, do my
own thing. But ... I think I want to keep playing. Mrs.
Rosenthal said she'd give us lessons together over the
summer two for one. We haven't done much together."
I felt shy all of a sudden. "If you'd like to."

Dad hugged me. "I'd love to. I miss spending a few
hours a week on a 'foolish waste of time.' And I'm keeping *this*—" he lifted up the pigtail photo and kissed it
before setting it back down—"here!"

We laughed together, and I took out a piece of my
music and we played a song together, stops and starts
and a couple of squeals, but ten minutes later we
laughed and clapped at ourselves.

Mom and Jake came home, and Jake looked at me
before he got into his truck to drive off with his friends.
I winked. Everything was okay.

We chatted together for a while, just trying to get a
normal feeling back into our family, and after it did I
went into my room and logged onto my email. There
was a note from Ellen.

> *Hey,*
>
> *I didn't hear from you after your lesson. I didn't
> call, thinking maybe things were stressful. I just
> wanted you to know that I quit the Yacht Club
> today. The summer would be no fun without you.*

*I'd been offered a part-time job baby-sitting the lit-
tle kid next door. I thought, why not? Then I can
spend time at the Jewish Community Center with
my best friend, Rachel. If she's not too busy eating
Spanish peanuts and counting backward with
Antonio Banderas, that is.*

> *Talk with you soon,*
> *E*

I could hardly believe it. Ellen had given up *her* job
for me! What a great, great friend. Summer was looking
good again.

Next email was from Kylie. The subject line read,
"Church Tomorrow!!"

Oh no! I quickly scanned it.

Hi there!
 *I'm so glad you can still come. Don't forget to be
at my house by like twenty till nine because I don't
want to be late. I'm s-s-s-scared! But so glad you'll
be there. See you soon!*

> *Daisies forever,*
> *Kylie*

In my great relief over the situation with my dad, I'd
completely forgotten I had promised to go to church
with Kylie. I emailed her back.

*Kylie—important news. I can't come in the morn-
ing. I'm sorry! Please call me so I know you got this
message.*

> *Daisies forever,*

Rachel

I called her but her voice mail came on right away. I didn't leave a message. What if she never turned her phone on before tomorrow morning? We needed to talk in person!

Her phone was either off or her battery had run down again. I didn't have her mom's number. Who could I call to get it?

I looked at my clock. Ten-thirty! I couldn't call anyone to get the number and couldn't call her mom at this hour anyway, either. Not only couldn't I be the kind of supportive friend Ellen was, but Kylie was going to think I stood her up.

I just couldn't let her down. I wouldn't.

Maybe I should just go to church this *one* time. Once wouldn't kill me, or Dad. Maybe Jake would drive me for five dollars.

CHAPTER ELEVEN
kylie's story

Maiden's Wreath *Francoa ramosa*
An easy plant that flowers year after year, this ever-green thrives in dappled sun and sandy soils. A vigorous plant that provides delicate and beautiful cut flowers. Blooms begin in late June.
>   —Northwest Gardener's Guide

Do you think Marian got a maiden's wreath in the end?
>   —Kylie Peterson

I stood in the driveway, waiting. Still no sign of Rachel. Finally I turned my phone on and dialed her number.

She answered. "Kylie!"

"Hey, where are you?" I could feel the sweat starting to gather at my pits.

There was a long silence. "I can't come," Rachel finally said. "My dad said no, and after thinking about it all night, I can't disobey. I'm so sorry. I'll fill you in on the details later."

I felt like crying, but I squeezed it back. I had to go anyway. It was my only chance.

"I'm sorry," Rachel said. "I'm really sorry."

"No problem," I mumbled, trying to be as positive as possible. It's not like it was her fault. "I'll talk with you later."

I grabbed the plastic bag of dyed daisies I had stayed up all night making and my tiny New Testament and headed toward Sarah's car, which had just pulled into the driveway. Mom had already gone to drop off the ad copy at the dealership, and Hayley had spent the night at a friend's house. I wished I could run back into the house. But I couldn't.

I opened the car door and scooted next to Sarah. "Rachel can't come." I didn't say more than that. It wasn't my story.

Sarah reached over and squeezed my hand. "Well, *I'll* be there, and so will lots of other people."

I nodded, not wanting to cry with her parents in the car or get all worked up before I had to stand in front of all these strangers and talk.

"They're going to think I'm weird," I said.

She shook her head. "No, they're not."

"It's a short talk."

"Even better." She smiled her encouragement at me, and I felt it warm me. It was good to have a best friend.

When we pulled up to the church, her mom and dad said good-bye and went into the sanctuary while we went to the middle school classroom in the chapel. Ben was at the door, greeting people along with the class teachers.

"Kylie! You came."

I nodded. "Did you think I'd ditch you?"

He shook his head. "Nah, but I need to talk with you first." He pulled me aside and told me that he'd sent an email to the camp and had just heard back last night. They just couldn't waive the requirement for teachers and counselors to have been a Christian for at least a year. "I'm so sorry about the counseling job—they've been asked to overlook that requirement before and just couldn't."

"I understand," I said. *Why* was I here? I couldn't be a counselor, and Rachel couldn't hear me explain my faith—in order to see it more clearly herself, I'd hoped.

"You don't have to talk today if you don't want to," Ben said.

"It's the right thing to do." I said it before I meant it. Then I did mean it. Suddenly I realized I was doing the right thing because I wanted to, not because anyone expected it of me or would think I was a bad person or not nice if I didn't.

I dug deep and found a smile and then set my bag of flowers by the speaker's podium.

This was the first time I'd been back in church since I'd talked with Jesus about being my Shepherd. It was different. Even though I knew hardly anyone, I felt like I belonged. None of my family went here, but it felt like *my* church much more than Gramps' church did.

Maybe churches didn't belong to people. Maybe they all belonged to God and whomever He invited or whoever came.

After the singing time it was sharing time. I went third. Sarah smiled encouragingly at me.

I steadied myself and the bag of flowers, but my voice rattled just a tiny bit. "Hi, my name is Kylie Peterson."

I looked out over the crowd of faces, some smiling, some kinda bored.

"I'm friends with Sarah"—I looked down and smiled at her—"and she first invited me to this church. She also invited me to apply to be a camp counselor with her this summer. She thought I was a Christian. *I* thought I was a Christian. I thought anyone who did good things and was nice to others and was kind and who went to church a couple of times a year was a Christian. Well, now I know that you have to choose to be a Christian. Ben was telling me that God knocks and we have to answer. I heard Him knock. A couple of weeks ago, I finally figured out what the noise was all about and I answered."

Almost everyone laughed at that. Next I smiled and shared my illustration about the flowers. "Anyone who wants one of the flowers can take one. I made a whole bunch."

"So, to finish up, I just want to say that because I haven't been a Christian for a year, I have to miss camp counseling this year. I hope you'll have me next year, and I'm just really glad to be a part of this church. Thanks."

I could see Sarah's eyes grow moist as I sat back down next to her. The lady teacher handed out my flowers to the many hands stuck out wanting one. That felt good. A few other kids, junior counselors, went to speak, and then it was time for the lesson. Half an hour later, church was over.

Ben came up. "You did a great job. And"—he slapped his forehead—"I can't believe I didn't think of this before. There aren't any requirements for the social get-togethers, the parties, or the game nights," Ben said. "Would you like to come to those? You'll get to have a good time and meet lots of people that you can work with *next* year!"

Goose bumps ran up my arm. Sarah looked at me. "Well?"

"Well, *yes*!" I said. It wouldn't solve my money problems, but how fun to hang out with these guys on some of the summer weekends. "I guess I won't have to roast marshmallows over candlelight in my kitchen after all!"

We all laughed.

"Your sister, Hayley, is welcome to camp any of the weeks that she wants to come at the reduced rate," Ben said. "Since you'll be counseling there next year, after all."

Hayley would be psyched. "Thanks so much. It will mean the world to her."

After church lots of the girls came up, with their flowers, to tell me how cool the lesson was. Then I went to get Sarah—to drag her away from some guy who I suspected was Sarah's crush—and then her parents took us home.

When I got there, there was a car in my driveway. Whose car was that?

"Would you like me to wait while you see who it is before we leave?" Sarah's dad asked.

I nodded.

When I ran up the driveway, Rachel hopped out of the other car. "Kylie!" she ran toward me. "I'm *so* sorry about this."

I nodded to Sarah's parents that this was okay, they could leave. They tooted their horn as a goodbye and headed home.

"You didn't have to drive over here," I said.

"How did it go?"

"Really good." I told her that I couldn't have the job but that I could hang with them at the social things.

"I quit my job, too," she said. "I'll fill you in on the details later. I'm sorry about this morning, but my dad didn't want me to come. He felt uncomfortable with the church thing. At least for now."

I hadn't even thought of that. "I'm sorry. I didn't even think that might be awkward."

A motorcycle rounded the corner and made it hard to hear.

"I wish my mom were here so your dad could meet her," I said, speaking a bit more loudly above the motorcycle engine. I wished it would go away. I wanted Mr. Cohen to like me and my neighborhood. *Good grief.*

The motorcycle pulled into my driveway!

My *mother* was driving it!

She turned the bike off and removed her helmet. I saw Mr. Cohen roll down the automatic passenger window. He looked at Rachel and raised his eyebrows. Rachel looked at me as my *mother* got off the bike.

"Um, hello, I'd like you to meet my mother," I said to Mr. Cohen.

"Janet Peterson." She shook his hand.

"Mom," I said. "What *is* this?"

"The dealership wanted the ad copy—and has signed me to do a few more. They even loaned me the bike for a day—and two helmets—for a signing bonus." Her eyes twinkled. "You *did* say you wanted to ride a motorcycle, didn't you?"

Rachel and I hooked hands and jumped up and down. Even Rachel's dad laughed out loud.

"I'll email you," Rachel said. "And you're coming to Jed and Davina's party next month, right?"

"Right!" I could barely concentrate. We were going biking!

I waved good-bye to the Cohens, brought my purse and Bible into the house, and quickly changed clothes.

When I was ready, my mom and I each slipped on a black and pink helmet, and then I got on the back of the bike and we backed down the driveway.

I started humming "Born to Be Wild." I don't think anyone heard me.

Oh, except God.

A few weeks later I sat on the large lawn at Aunt Beth and Uncle Andy's house. There must have been hundreds of people there—spilling across the front lawn, milling about the back in the nursery area. A dozen newly graduated kindergartners somersaulted down the hill to the side of the house. My dog, Missy, was in heaven.

I lounged against the carpet of grass, sipping my lemonade. Rachel would be here soon.

Would Jake come?

Aunt Beth came and sat down with me. "Hey, you."

"Hey, you," I said.

"Enjoying the party? Hungry?"

I nodded. "Davina looks as beautiful a bride in jeans as she was in her wedding dress!"

Aunt Beth laughed. "Yes. Jed can't take his eyes off of her. Hey," her voice grew more serious, "I heard you lost your summer job."

I nodded. "Did you hear why?"

Aunt Beth nodded. "Your mother told me. But their bad news is my good news—if you're willing."

I sat up. "What do you mean?"

"Leeann is staying in Canada this summer to take some extra classes. I'll need some help at the nursery. Usually she was a full-time summer worker, but I thought maybe you, and maybe Rachel, would each like to work here part time." Aunt Beth's face wrinkled into smiles. "It'd be such a waste not to use any of that plant knowledge you've been gathering."

"Really?" I said. "You'd really want us? Is it okay with my mom?"

She nodded. "Rachel's mom, too. They'll take turns driving you guys up here, and I'll drive you home. It's hard work." Aunt Beth flexed her biceps. "But good money—and buff arms."

Flubba, say good-bye.

"I'd love it!" I said. When she told me what she was going to pay me, my eyes bugged. It was more than the counseling job. Weekends off, of course. The chance to hang with my family—and Rachel, too, sometimes. I hoped.

Just then Rachel's car pulled up. I hugged Aunt Beth. "Thank you! I'm going to talk with Rachel about it!"

Someone strummed guitar across the lawn, and a warm breeze ran through my carefully done hair as I raced toward the Cohens' car.

Rachel's dad and her mom got out. Then Rachel. No Jake.

She came up to me. "Isn't it cool? I knew yesterday, but I told your aunt I'd keep the secret till she could talk to you."

"It *is* cool," I said. We walked together toward the barbecue and sat down at one of the picnic tables scattered around the grounds. We chattered for a while and made plans, and she told me how much she wanted me to meet her friend Ellen. I said we'd definitely get together—maybe with Sarah, all four of us.

"I'm going to get some more lemonade," she said. "Want some?"

I shook my head. "Had enough, thanks."

I watched the white daisies, big and small, bobbing all around the fields. *Thanks for letting me share that at church,* I told God inside my head. *But since camp is off for now, I feel kind of bad that now that I really do know you and am learning more about you every day, I have no one to share my exciting discoveries with.*

I looked up. My eyes were drawn toward Hayley—showing off her ballet to the younger kids from Davina's class. My mom clapped.

Well, those two, of course, I told God.

I heard Rachel's laugh from across the field.

Oh yes. And Rachel, too. Thank you. Thank you!

I felt two hands clasp over my eyes. I knew who it was before I looked.

It was Jake. My heart jumped.

"Hey." He sat down next to me.

"Hi," I said. "I thought you weren't coming." *Uh-oh, gave away that I'd been looking for him.*

"I'm not staying," he said. "I'm working. But I wanted to stop by. Bubbie doesn't feel good, and she sent me to take a picture of the bride and groom for the collection on her piano."

I nodded. After a minute I asked, "Everything okay between us?"

Jake smiled, and his bright blue eyes crinkled. "Yeah. Can't say I'm not disappointed, but I understand. Parents exist to make rules." He laughed. "And they're not all bad. How do you feel?"

"Disappointed, but right," I said. "I'll be seventeen in just a few years." I let my eyes twinkle at him. Born to be wild and all that.

He winked as he stood up. "I'll remember that. I'm sure I'll see you around." At that moment I felt only good things for him, and I think he did for me, too.

As he began to leave, he turned and lightly tossed something at me. "It's for your hair, *Katriel*." I caught it. He watched me set it on my Maid Marian hairdo, winked, and walked away.

A wreath of the tiniest daisy chains.

Katriel, the Hebrew blessing name that Davina had given me. How did Jake know about that? I smiled as I remembered what *Katriel* meant.

God is my crown.

If your first concern is to look after yourself,
you'll never find yourself. But if you forget
about yourself and look to me,
you'll find both yourself and me.

Matthew 10:39 THE MESSAGE

Connect with other FRIENDS FOR A SEASON readers at *www.FriendsforaSeason.com*!

- Sign up for Sandra Byrd's newsletter
- Send e-cards to your friends
- Download FRIENDS FOR A SEASON wallpapers and icons
- Get a sneak peek at upcoming books in the series
- Learn more about the places and events featured in each book

www.FriendsforaSeason.com

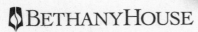

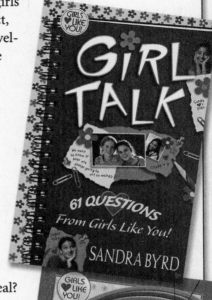